PS 3565
.D59
P47

PS 3565 .D59 P47

O'Donnell, Lillian

The phone calls

MAY 1992

OCT '87

JUN 82

KALAMAZOO VALLEY COMMUNITY COLLEGE
LEARNING RESOURCES CENTER
KALAMAZOO, MICHIGAN 49009

31557

# The Phone Calls

*By the same author*

**THE FACE OF THE CRIME**

**THE TACHI TREE**

# The Phone Calls

by Lillian O'Donnell

HODDER AND STOUGHTON
LONDON · SYDNEY · AUCKLAND · TORONTO

*Copyright © 1972 by Lillian O'Donnell. First printed in Great Britain 1972. ISBN 0 340 16556 1. Reproduced from the original setting by arrangement with G.P. Putnam's Sons. All rights reserved. No part of this publication may be reproduced or transmitted in any form or by any means, electronic or mechanical, including photocopy, recording, or any information storage and retrieval system, without permission in writing from the publisher. Printed in Great Britain for Hodder and Stoughton Limited, St. Paul's House, Warwick Lane, London EC4P 4AH, by Compton Printing Limited, London and Aylesbury.*

# Chapter 1

No matter how late she left it, dawdling along the half-dark city streets, how long she paused at each lighted shopwindow, no matter how she postponed it, ultimately she would have to go home. She would reach the canopied entrance, walk through the foyer to the automatic elevator, punch the button, and, swaddled in a cocoon of hushed canned music, be lifted up to the eighth floor. The softly lit, flower-carpeted passage would be silent and vacant as always. Her footsteps would be absorbed in that soundproof vacuum lock between the world outside and the tight individual microcosms behind the row of padlocked doors. Inevitably, she would reach her own door and have no choice but to go inside—

To emptiness. To a silence that was so overwhelming no raucous street noise or blare of radio could alleviate it.

In the three years she and Clem had lived in the Hampton Towers she had not encountered another tenant in the hall more than half a dozen times. If she'd thought about it then, she would have shrugged. In fact, there'd been a period when this insularity of New York apartment living had suited her. Not now. Now Ruth Emerson, the weariness of unused hours dragging her steps, would have given a great deal for the sight of one of her neighbors, for the most inane of social exchanges. She hadn't spoken to anyone but Lamarr, the doorman, and the waitress at Schrafft's in four days.

At least, she reminded herself fumbling in her purse for the key, she didn't have to be afraid anymore. Yet as she entered into the irrevocable silence of her apartment, she tensed automatically against the muffled ringing of the telephone which might shatter it.

But there was only the steady hum of the air conditioner underscoring the loneliness. Putting on the hall light, she caught a glimpse of herself in the console mirror. It no longer shocked her to see her white face haggard and crazed with new lines, defeated eyes, blond hair dingy and lank with the betraying dark roots. She'd never been pretty, but she'd had a good figure and a contagious vivacity. Exuberance, enthusiasm, those had been her trademarks. Thirty-five, she had passed for twenty-eight. She'd never look like that again.

She couldn't have begun to imagine what it would be like without Clem—permanently. He had been away a lot—that was the start of the trouble: There had been so much solitary waiting. Now there wasn't anyone or anything to wait for.

Clem's boss had come himself to break the news. As soon as Ruth saw Charles Staff at the door, she knew the worst. It needed only the details, and they were not really important. Clem had been on an upstate swing, driving over the mountains to Saratoga. He'd covered the route plenty of times before, knew the narrow roads well, but on this occasion the fog had been heavy; somehow he'd missed the turn and gone over the edge. What mattered was that Clem, her husband, was dead.

The company had spared her as much as possible, made all the arrangements about bringing the body back to New York. When she went down to the funeral parlor to see her husband, the mortician advised her, "Best not, Mrs. Emerson." With the first uneasy stirrings of guilt she hadn't insisted.

But distracted by the details with which death encumbers the living, she was able for a while to put away the doubts.

When Clement Emerson in his closed casket was finally lowered into the ground, when Mr. Staff and the salesmen and secretaries walked away from the graveside, then Ruth Emerson had to face herself. She hadn't heard from Julio and didn't want to. It wasn't his fault, but she would never see him again. Regret intensified her grief, and the small nagging uncertainty grew.

She fell into listlessness, lying in bed till one or two in the afternoon, getting up to make black coffee and toast and to start the day's chain-smoking. She threw on clothes to go down to the Schrafft's on the corner for dinner, then back to chain-smoke in front of the television set. Sometimes she fell asleep in the chair. She stopped cleaning her home or herself. There were no relatives on either side to comfort her, and anyhow she wouldn't have confided her real distress to anyone. So Ruth Emerson continued for what was to her an indeterminate period but in actuality only eight days. Then one morning she awoke and recognized the reality of the shambles in which she was existing. She forced herself to eat a decent breakfast, to resume a regular routine of housekeeping, and to bring some order about her own person. Clem had been killed on April 30—a dark, rainy, terrible day. By the middle of May the weather turned balmy, and that helped.

She had been on the edge of recovery when the telephone calls began.

At first there was only silence on the line, so she hung up, thinking it was a wrong number. But it happened so often that it began to upset her.

"Who is this? Please? What number do you want? Who are you? Why are you doing this?"

There was no answer to her pleading. Then one endless night the calls had come ineluctably every hour till at dawn, distraught beyond fear, she'd taken the receiver off the hook for a few hours of fitful sleep. Upon waking, as soon as she'd put the receiver back, the phone had rung—instantly.

She answered.

"Don't do that again."

His voice was low, husky, its raw emotionalism overlaid with cultured diction, and that added to the horror. "Don't ever take your phone off the hook again, Ruth. You hear me? You hear me?"

"Yes, I hear you."

"Then don't ever do it again. Don't make me angry, Ruth, I warn you, or you'll be sorry."

"Who are you? Why are you doing this? Please, why are you doing this to me?"

"Say it. I want you to say it—I won't ever take the phone off the hook again."

"I won't ever take the phone off the hook again," she repeated in a whimper, knowing that she would not have the courage to break that promise. "But please, who are you?"

There was a pause. "A friend of your husband."

"Of Clem? What's your name?"

"Why? What do you have in mind, Ruth?" And there followed a string of sly and ugly innuendos, insinuations about her past to which were added obscene suggestions for the future. She couldn't speak, listening till he chose to stop, her hand still holding the receiver after the line went dead.

That was the way it began. After that, a call might come at any hour of the day or night. She was constantly on edge waiting, jumping at the slightest sound, and the actual ring of the telephone was enough to bring on a crying jag. Too ashamed to go to the police, she finally reached a plateau of exhaustion and with it a temporary lucidity enabling her to contact the telephone company.

They were very matter-of-fact about it. In a way that was calming; the offense must be ordinary, many women similarly harassed if the phone company sent out a printed questionnaire. In due time it arrived. She was asked to keep a record of the calls for a week and then mail it back. As she read through the list, she realized that her case was not ordinary after all—the caller knew too much about her, about Clem, and about. . . . She tore up the paper and asked the telephone company to arrange for a new and unlisted number.

Since that time, for a period of four days the phone hadn't rung.

Yet as Ruth Emerson crossed the dark living room, she felt the familiar tightening of her stomach, the pains of fear. *Relax. It's over. He can't get to you anymore.* She forced herself to breathe slowly and deeply, felt the cramps ease.

Just the same, the first thing she looked at after turning on the bedroom lights was the telephone on the night table. Should she take it off the hook tonight just to make sure? These past four nights she'd lain awake waiting. . . . If she could get one really full night's sleep, maybe she'd feel well enough and look decent enough to go out and start looking for work.

She was perspiring. Then she realized that the room was very still. The air conditioner had stopped. It was not yet June, not hot enough for the air conditioner, but she used it so the windows could stay closed and she could keep the city grime out. So now Ruth Emerson pushed up the center of the bank of three wall-to-wall windows and stood for a moment enjoying the cool spring breeze. Then she pulled down the bedspread, folded it, and placed it neatly aside on its rack. Turning down the covers, she plumped up the pillows in preparation for reading. She felt calmer. Maybe a glass of milk would help. She started for the kitchen.

The phone rang.

She stopped where she was. It rang again. She turned to look at it in dismay.

Was she really hearing it, or was it a trick of her nerves? She hadn't given the new number out to anyone, not anyone at all. Could it be the phone company calling? She glanced at the clock—not after eleven at night. Could it be someone for the person who had had the number before her? There was always that possibility; the company had warned her of it. Well, if so, the ringing would soon stop.

It didn't.

Ruth Emerson walked toward the instrument as though mesmerized. Circling the bed, she picked up the receiver and held it to her ear gingerly. She didn't speak—it wasn't necessary.

"Hello, Ruth." He sounded almost friendly. "Ruth?" he prodded as she remained incapable of answering.

"How did you get this number?" she asked finally with the flatness of resignation.

"It's jotted right there on the telephone pad."

It took a moment for that to filter through the numbness. "You mean—Oh, God! You mean you were here, in my apartment, in my bedroom?"

"You have a nice place, very. I like it. I'll be coming again. I can't say when, but soon . . . soon. . . ." He went on telling her how it would be, what he would do . . . what she would do. . . .

Joseph Antony Capretto arrived on the scene within three minutes of receiving the call. He'd been in the area interviewing the owner of a restaurant on York Avenue whose bartender had been shot the night before during a robbery. At this time of night in this kind of neighborhood—half-commercial, half-residential—there shouldn't be much of a crowd on the street. As soon as he turned the corner of Fifty-fifth, he noted the small knot of spectators. He was glad he'd been right—it made one less problem. Just the same it was sad to see how little interest the violent destruction of a human being stirred in the city. Not so long ago violence hadn't been taken for granted, not so long ago there had been no fear about extending sympathy or showing pity. Joe double parked in front of the Hampton Towers marquee and got out.

"Police officer, stand aside, please." The curious parted with alacrity and just as quickly closed in behind him. "Capretto, Homicide." He flashed his ID for the patrolman guarding the covered form on the pavement.

"Coogan," the officer identified himself in return. His Adam's apple jumped in his long neck, but his tensely hunched shoulders dropped an inch with relief at the arrival of someone of higher rank capable of shouldering responsibility. "You're the first, Sergeant."

"No, Coogan, you are," Joe Capretto corrected. "You procure that and put it over her?" He pointed to the worn piece of plaid blanket.

The shoulders hunched again, defensively. "Yes, sir."

Capretto had already moved around to the head and was lifting a corner of the blanket. His mouth stretched in a grimace that pulled the beginnings of a double chin back into a taut, hard jawline. He swallowed but lifted the covering a little higher so he could see the rest of her. Then gently he replaced it.

"You did right, Coogan." He looked around. "Anybody make a try at identification?"

"Yes, Sergeant, the doorman."

Coogan indicated a tall, thin youth with hair curling bushily from the edges of his uniform cap and sideburns inching hopefully down toward a round, childishly pudgy chin. His face had lost every bit of color so that the bumps and blemishes turned it into a moon map. Behind gold-rimmed glasses his eyes reflected sickness at what he had seen.

"He says it's a Mrs. Ruth Emerson from 8B. He recognized the dress and the brooch. It was what she was wearing when she came in about twenty-five minutes before . . . before the accident," Coogan finished uncertainly. "Also, that's her window up there."

There was no need for Joe to lift the blanket again; he remembered the distinctive Maltese cross in silver that had been pinned to the front of the victim's black dress. He did step out to the edge of the sidewalk to look up to where Coogan pointed. All the windows of the building but that one were closed, drapes revealing a line of light here and there. As though to underline the contrast, the sheer white curtains billowed out in a sudden gust of wind. Joe beckoned to the doorman.

"Have you tried getting Mrs. Emerson on the house phone? I suppose there is a house phone?"

"Oh, yes, sir, oh, yes there is. But I never thought—"

"Do it now. Go and buzz her apartment."

In the distance the ambulance whined its approach, screeched turning the corner from Second Avenue, and came to an abrupt but smooth stop behind the sergeant's car. A white-clad figure, kit in hand, bounded out of the rear, sprinted, then knelt beside the form on the pavement. He raised the faded piece of blanket at the head more briskly than Capretto had done, pulling it half off with professional matter-of-factness. He stopped abruptly, winced, then frowned to cover his unprofessional reaction. The groan from the crowd stiffened him.

Joe jerked his head at Patrolman Coogan, who immediately stepped forward with the familiar incantation: "Move along, move along now. It's all over. Move along, please...."

"Got your pictures yet, Sergeant?" The intern looked up at Joe. The crowd had been more or less dispersed—the intern could permit himself a sigh. "Well, there's no rush. No rush."

"No." Capretto agreed, taking one more look, a long one this time, and like the young doctor, he didn't try to hide the sadness and revulsion it caused him. Then he turned and went into the vestibule of the Hampton Towers, where the doorman stood before a bank of name plates and push buttons set into the wall.

"Any answer?"

"No, sir."

"You've got a pass key?"

"Yes, sir."

"What's your name?"

"Bernstein. Lamarr Bernstein."

"Okay, Mr. Bernstein, let's go up."

They rode in the paneled and carpeted elevator letting the innocuous music wash over them. Joe said nothing, not that he didn't have questions, he had plenty, but it didn't seem right to ask them to the accompaniment of a Sigmund Romberg medley. Anyhow, he wanted a look at the scene first.

Bernstein led him down the silent hallway of blank doors to the one marked 8B.

"This is it," he croaked and started to insert the pass key.

"Hold it." Capretto pressed the bell button. "Just to make sure." They could hear the faint ringing inside, but no answering voice or movement. Joe rang again. "Okay," he told Bernstein.

They went in. The light was on in the foyer, but the living room beyond was dark. The reflections from the street filtering through the sheer curtains and the square of light from the open bedroom combined to make passage across the room possible without the danger of bumping into anything. The tenant, of course, would hardly need even that much visibility.

"Mrs. Emerson?" Joe called out. "Anybody home? It's the police, Mrs. Emerson. Don't be frightened."

No answer.

"There's a switch around here someplace . . ."

"No!" Capretto barked, pushing Bernstein's hand aside. "Don't touch anything. I want to get the picture just the way it was."

He started toward the bedroom. The point was that Ruth Emerson in coming home had gone straight through to her bedroom. So at the threshold Sergeant Joe Capretto, Homicide North, paused. He seemed as he stood poised a very physical man—good-looking, relaxed, indulgent of his body's pleasures. Always stocky, lately he'd put on considerable weight, but a lot of him was still muscle. He made it a point to work out regularly. Only a very unperceptive miscreant would underrate his fitness. But Joseph Antony also had the Latin's emotional intuition. Even Lamarr Bernstein sensed it in the narrowing of the sergeant's thickly lashed, dark eyes as they assessed the room, in the frown of concentration that jumped the bridge of his nearly perfect Roman nose. He was picking up a taint of corruption in that room that reached beyond a woman's taking her own life. Capretto's dark face darkened further.

At the same time his ordinary senses were making their routine notations. To start: This was in fact the open window he'd seen from the street, its curtains now limply still—he could tell by the relation of the buildings on the other side—and the room was empty. It was well-furnished, imitation French Provincial but of good quality—a feminine room, the chairs upholstered in a pale-blue watery silk matching the valence above the curtains and also probably matching the bedspread which had been removed and was neatly folded inside out on its rack. . . .

The bed was turned down.

The covers were turned back in a precise triangle to show pale-blue sheets, pillows plumped up invitingly, robe and nightgown laid out at the foot of the bed. Joe's frown deepened. Why should a woman who intended to jump out the window get her bed ready like that? If she'd meant to put herself permanently to sleep by taking an overdose of sleeping pills or even poison, then the meticulous preparations would make sense. As it was. . . . Joe's eyes roamed to the night table. The telephone receiver dangled by its cord.

At last Joe entered the bedroom.

Using his pocket handkerchief, he picked up the receiver and listened. Nobody on the line. He replaced the receiver; then taking a deep breath and slowly letting it out, he picked up the phone once more and dialed.

"Operator, this is Sergeant Capretto, Homicide. I'm at. . . ." He looked at the number plate set in the base. "Wait a minute, it's been scratched out and another number . . . 219-5343. The receiver was off the hook. Can you check for me if there was any traceable call made from this number or to it in the past hour or so?"

"I'll have to get the supervisor for that." The metallic, mechanical response was anything but helpful.

"Of course, I understand." They kidded him—Brennan, David Link, all the guys, even the lieutenant—about his middle-aged spread. They said being the only son with all his sisters married, his mother was spoiling him. They said he'd lose his touch with the women, and a younger man would soon be taking over those choice assignments that had gone to him as a matter of course. So now Joe radiated charm over the wire. "I know I'm putting you to a lot of trouble, Miss. . . ." He waited.

"Smith." Then almost involuntarily she added, "Lorraine."

"Ah, Lorraine," he repeated, savoring its syllables. "A beautiful name. Do what you can for me, will you, Miss Smith, and call me back. Okay?"

Her flustered "Oh, well, sure, I'll try. I want to help, naturally, if I can . . ." indicated the message had registered.

Joe stared at the mutilated number plate. "And if you could check whether this number has been changed recently, I'd be really grateful."

He hung up. It was all much more effort than it used to be and much less exhilarating. He took a deep breath, and with the subsequent heave to clear his lungs, Joe, who had once nearly made the Olympic track team, turned to question the doorman. These first questions were often the most important, the ones that set the tenor of the whole case. Often the first facts to be elicited were the foundation of the ultimate solution, or so Joe had found it. Therefore, he took an extra few seconds to prepare.

Bernstein fidgeted.

"You told Officer Coogan that you saw Mrs. Emerson come into the lobby about twenty-five minutes before . . . her death. Was she alone?"

"Yes, sir."

"How can you be so sure of the time?"

"I had my transistor on to the eleven o'clock news. Then the sports cast came on, and it was still on when she fell."

Capretto looked at the scrawny young man sharply. "Very good. Now, when she entered the building, did she speak to you?"

"She said good night."

*She couldn't have been too preoccupied then,* Joe thought. "That's all? Did she seem worried or upset?"

"No, sir. No more than usual."

"Oh? How's that?"

"Well, you see, her husband died recently; he was killed in an automobile accident like . . . well, actually it was the end of April . . . yeah, that's right. She took it real hard. She kind of holed up in that apartment for . . . like . . . maybe a couple of weeks. Then when she finally showed, she was a mess. I mean, she really was. She used to be a real looker, for a woman her age, but you wouldn'a known her when she came out. Me and the super, Mr. Carruthers, we talked about it, but it wasn't none of our business, naturally."

"Naturally." Joe suppressed a sigh. "Did she have a job? Did she go to work before her husband's death?"

"Nope, she didn't do a thing. I think maybe she meant to look for work because the last three or four nights she'd been coming in from her meal with the early edition of the *Times* folded to the help wanted ads."

Observant, Joe thought again, and curious—all to the good. "Did Mrs. Emerson have many visitors since her husband's death? You're supposed to announce all visitors before letting them go up, aren't you?" He added it only to forestall any righteous protestations.

"Yeah, I am, and I do; but there weren't any. Not before and not after. Though there were a few right around the time of the funeral."

"How about friends in the building?"

"I only know who comes in and who goes out; I don't know about what goes on inside."

Was that a hint that there was plenty going on inside? "She never spoke about any of the other tenants?"

"No, sir. She kept herself to herself. Always did, like the rest of them. Oh, they smile all right, and say good morning, nice day, and like that, but they don't really see you."

Not a hint, only the resentment that was so prevalent and open these days. Again Joe took that characteristic deep breath and heaved the air out again. He walked over to the window. The sill was low, just above his knees, but it would have caught Ruth Emerson higher; also, there was a broad ledge outside. Because of its width, Joe, craning forward cautiously, could not see his car or the ambulance parked at the curb directly below—that meant the fall could not have been an accident. By placing himself sideways at the window's corner, he could spot the row of cars double parked in front of the building; it appeared that not only the technical crew but the precinct people and the DA's men had arrived. The added brightness in the street indicated spotlights had been set up. For a moment Joe ignored the turmoil there now and tried to visualize the street as it must have been in the earlier quiet of a Sunday night before Ruth Emerson went over that wide ledge to spatter on the sidewalk.

Directly opposite the Hampton Towers was a garage only two stories high, but to the right was a modern apartment building the same height as the Towers. The windows were all open now as the tenants gaped at the unusual activity. But had they been earlier? Still, someone while either raising or lowering a shade just might have caught a glimpse of Ruth Emerson, might have seen a second person in the room with her. The sooner those people in the front apartments were interrogated, the better. Joe turned back into the quiet, lamplit room with its middle-class luxury and the inviting solace of that turned-down bed.

The phone rang.

He picked it up as carefully as before, waiting for the caller to speak first.

"Oh, Miss Smith." He relaxed. "You're really terrific! You're a real fast worker; I didn't expect to hear from you this soon. . . ." He listened to her gratification and then waited through her apologies. "Well, you did your best. . . . Yes, I realize you can't trace a dial call. . . . I realize you wouldn't know the receiver was off the hook unless someone reported not being able to get through. . . . The number is unlisted, so without special access you have no way of knowing when it was changed? . . . Well, I certainly appreciate. . . ." Now he couldn't turn her off. "You've been so nice, I wonder if you'd do one more thing for me? Check any toll calls to or from the number in—say, the past week? Would you? You're a doll, Miss Lorraine, a real doll."

He didn't think it would be significant, but it was the only way he could think of ending the conversation, and of course, one never knew. Maybe he *was* getting flabby and comfortable, but he could still turn it on with the ladies.

Briskly, Joe hung up and, walking into the living room, flicked on the main light switch. A quick search revealed a clutter of unpaid bills, sympathy notes whose formal tone indicated they were not from close friends, and an address book with remarkably few entries. It failed to uncover what he was looking for. Not that he'd expected it to. If Ruth Emerson had written a suicide note at the desk, she would have needed light and she would have left that light on so the note could be found.

Joe went back to the bedroom to stare again at the neatly turned-down bed and the white telephone beside it. She might have put the call in herself to say a final good-bye to someone before jumping, but then she would not have meticulously turned down the covers and laid out her nightgown and robe. If someone had pushed her, surely he would not have done it while she was talking on the phone. So the call itself had to be the cause of death.

It could have been bad news. Someone called and gave Ruth Emerson bad news. Still partially in shock over her husband's sudden death, desolate and alone, it had been more than she could bear.

Joe Capretto sighed. He felt sorry for all the lonely people, the ones who had no one with whom to share sorrow, or joy for that matter.

# Chapter 2

Norah knew her father was up; she also knew that as soon as he heard them in the hall, he'd turn out the lights, scurry to his own room, and shut the door, pretending to be asleep. She could almost make out the sounds of the cane tapping and his lame foot dragging. Except that it was only her imagination because the new carpet muffled all sound. Anyhow, she knew perfectly well what he was up to and that if she knocked on his door, he'd go through an elaborate procedure of heaving up and down on the bed so that the springs would creak, yawning loudly, finally calling out drowsily, a whole routine of waking which fooled neither of them. He was trying to make it easy for Artie. She wondered if Artie Webster realized how much of an ally he had in her father?

She handed him her key. He opened the door a scant half foot, then handed it back.

"Good night, doll."

"Good night, Artie. I enjoyed the movie. Thanks."

She was tall, nearly his height, so all she had to do was tilt her chin slightly for the ritual kiss.

He was more insistent than usual. "It's still early, baby. Why don't I come in for a few minutes?"

Artie Webster was blond, tall, good-looking, breezy. There were always lots of laughs with Artie. Norah liked to laugh, to do crazy, spur-of-the-moment things, but sometimes she preferred to be quiet and serious. Somehow she could never really relax with Artie, couldn't share a silence with him. An old crony of her father's who'd been in vaudeville described it as "being on." Artie was *on* all the time. Did he ever take the grin off and give his face a rest, Norah wondered. She had a quick vision of Artie sleeping, eyes closed and still grinning.

"Not tonight, Artie. I'm tired and I'm on the eight a.m. tour tomorrow."

"One little nightcap, what do you say?" He'd stretched his arm across the doorway so she couldn't get by.

"I don't want to disturb Dad."

"You know your old dad isn't going to object."

Which was exactly right—their entrance and a little mild necking were exactly what Patrick Mulcahaney behind his closed door was waiting and listening for. "Not tonight, Artie."

Artie looked hard at her, his smile still there but just barely. "Or any night, right, Norah?"

"I'm sorry," she said and meant it.

"Don't worry about it." Dropping the arm that had barred her way, he forced the smile back to full force. "You can't win 'em all, I always say." Turning, he walked jauntily down the hall.

Watching him go, Norah felt a twinge of regret, but it was momentary. They hadn't been right for each other; she'd kept going with him only to please her father. She just wished that she'd been as honest as Artie in facing up to the situation. She slipped inside and turned on the lights. All at once she was hungry. She clumped to the kitchen making more noise than necessary, letting the refrigerator door slam shut as she got out the eggs and milk, rattling the frying pan, running the faucet full force for water for the coffee. Let's see if he can ignore all that! Ah, there! She could hear the tugging at the door, his soft muttering because it stuck as usual, then the louder expletive as it suddenly flew open, finally his shuffle on the bare corridor floor. She had to smile.

"Norah?"

He stood in the doorway, erect but for the slight list to the right as he leaned on the cane to ease the weight from his mangled left foot, a fine, vigorous, stocky man of sixty-five. His face, though crisscrossed with fine lines, was ruddy—Pat Mulcahaney believed in fresh air and was out in it two hours each day no matter what the weather. It was one of the reasons they still lived on Riverside Drive with its narrow band of park edging the Hudson below. Also, there was O'Flaherty's gym, where he worked out daily with the weights and pulleys, and Houlihan's Bar on the corner, where he refreshed himself after those exertions—as good a recipe for health and longevity as Pat Mulcahaney could offer any man. Not to mention that Mulcahaney had for years been a district captain. Though he was no longer active in the party, he wasn't about to lose the position of elder statesman by moving out of the neighborhood.

"What happened?" Pat asked his daughter.

"Nothing."

But something had; he could sense it. Pat Mulcahaney understood his daughter very well because she was like him: strong, self-reliant, to the point of stubbornness sometimes —all right, he admitted that for both of them. She even looked like him: tall, for a girl, built on fine, bold lines. Her face was broad and open with a clear high brow and large blue-gray eyes generously fringed and set widely apart. Her jaw was somewhat blunt, call it firm, and she had really white, even teeth—again like his. But though her jaw might be a little aggressive, Norah's mouth was soft and mobile like his dear dead Jenny's, and she had his wife's white, clear skin, and her luxuriant hair, a brown so darkly close to black as made no difference. Norah possessed all of her mother's sensitivity as well. That was the problem, the conflict of the two natures in the girl, and he had aggravated it by putting too much responsibility on her too soon.

Maybe he should have married again. During his wife's illness the household duties had devolved naturally on the twelve-year-old girl. He should have hired a housekeeper right then. He hadn't done it because it would have admitted that he knew Jenny was dying. Afterward, well, doing her mother's chores had seemed important to the child, a kind of therapy. She'd had such a fierce pride in her ability to run the house for him and the two boys. Bringing in another woman might have seemed a rejection. So he had reasoned. The truth was that he hadn't wanted another woman around —that for him the memory of Jenny was too dear. So Norah grew up bossing three men, and they'd played up to her, he and the boys, at first teasingly deferent till it became a habit for her to give orders and for them to obey.

The years melted away. Pat, Jr., and Michael went to Vietnam, came home, got jobs, and Norah graduated and prepared for college. Then the accident. A new man at the controls of the giant crane, the levers jamming, the monstrous maw crashing down on him. Norah never left his side. The college year began, and he was still bedridden. She was to stay only till he was mobile again. By the time he was self-sufficient, Norah claimed she'd lost interest. He didn't argue very hard, not believing in overeducated women anyway. Had he been selfish?

His guilt was strong enough so that when the boys married and moved West and there were just the two of them, Pat insisted she should get out into the world, get a job. It was not his ultimate desire for her, but it was a start. Late, but not too late—it was up to him to see to that. And he was trying, though he couldn't push too hard or he'd get the opposite reaction. Oh, yes! Patrick Mulcahaney knew his daughter as well as he knew himself.

Norah wouldn't look at him, only kept staring at the eggs in the frying pan.

"Have a nice time?" He tried again.

"It was a terrible picture."

"Why didn't you ask Artie in? It's not that late."

She hesitated, then decided she might as well tell him and get it over with. "We broke up."

"Why?"

She shrugged.

"I thought you liked him."

"I did . . . at first, but he was too . . . too much of a live wire for me. He was pushing all the time, selling. . . ."

"What do you expect? He's a salesman. A good one. A real hot shot. His boss told me he's the best time salesman the station has."

"You investigated him?"

"I didn't *investigate*. I'm not a policeman. I just asked a few fatherly pertinent questions."

"Before or after you brought him up to the house?"

"Before, naturally. Do you think I'd bring a stranger up to meet my daughter?"

His Irish indignation was so sincere Norah had a hard time stifling her laughter. "All right, but from now on you're to let me find my own boyfriends."

"Where? Where are you going to meet anybody, except criminals?" Patrick Mulcahaney roared.

"Dad!"

"You're so wrapped up in that job of yours and you keep such crazy hours. Since you joined the force, you haven't had a life of your own."

"Dad, I want you to promise not to pick up any more likely prospects on your park bench or down at district headquarters, and I'll promise not to be an old maid since that's what's worrying you."

"Sweetheart, that's the last thing I'm worried about. You're a sweet womanly woman, and you'll have dozens of offers as soon as you make up your mind you want them." Now they smiled at each other, the squabble over. "I just hope you don't wait too long before making it up." Now he'd gone and spoiled it again, hadn't been able to help it. He decided the only way to keep his mouth shut was to put something in it.

"Is there any beer left? I'll have a glass while you eat." Just as they were starting to relax with each other again, the extension phone rang. "Oh, hell and damnation! What do they want at this hour of the night?"

Norah's smile, tentative before, broadened. "I thought you said it wasn't late?"

"It's not for some things, much too late for others."

But Norah was already taking the call. "Yes, ma'am. No, ma'am, I'm still up, and I can leave right away. There's a subway stop at Fiftieth and Lex' so I can be there in about twenty minutes or half an hour depending on how long I have to wait for a train." She hung up.

"You're not on duty," Pat Mulcahaney protested.

"A woman jumped or fell to her death. Somebody has to search the body, and it has to be a woman—out of respect. You know that."

She was already out of the kitchen and picking up the lightweight spring coat she'd dropped on the hall chair. He called out. "Aren't you going to eat your eggs?"

"No time. You have them. And leave the dishes. I'll do them in the morning."

Mulcahaney hobbled to the doorway in time to catch her parting look—intent, serious, and excited. She was too involved in the job; she cared too much. He should never have let her join the force. It would take a real man to make her give it up. Evidently Artie Webster had not been the one. So he'd have to try a little harder. Maybe he'd give Pat Jr. and Mike a call, see if they knew any likely prospects. . . .

Norah's timing was good. She got to the scene just as the assistant medical examiner, a thin, intent young man she'd never seen before, was finishing. Then it was her turn—the duty being to search the body, removing personal effects to be turned over to the property clerk. The initial shock at seeing the condition of the victim was so great that Norah doubted she could go through with the search. What would happen if she couldn't bring herself to it? She must have hesitated longer than she realized because suddenly she

**FROM THE DESK OF**

**DONALD H. KILGORE, D.D.S.**
609 NORTHAMPTON ROAD
KALAMAZOO, MICHIGAN 49007

Telephone 345-1455

$240

(1) $29.95 10:00 a.m. Friday car @ Denoyer on Stadium

(2) $40.00 pay ticket & mail to station

(3) owe mom $20

(4) withdraw $150 for shopping

became aware that the young ME was looking at her. So she bit her lips, knelt, and began.

There was no purse, and the woman had had no money on her. She wore a thin, gold-plated, heart-shaped locket on a chain around her neck inside the high collar of the plain black dress. There was a picture of a man inside, in his mid-thirties perhaps, nice-looking, serious, and opposite was an inscription: "All my love, Clem." She wore a Maltese cross for a brooch, but the only other item was of greater value than the two combined—a heavy gold chain and filigree bracelet. Initials were engraved on the inside of the clasp, small and by the streetlight difficult to make out. In her handbag, besides the usual items and her service revolver, Norah also carried a clean white man's handkerchief. She placed the three pieces of jewelry inside and, knotting the corners, firmly placed the small bundle in her handbag.

"Where's the sergeant?" She looked around at the various officers, addressing no one in particular.

Coogan answered. "Upstairs. Apartment 8B."

"Thanks." She nodded and went into the building.

She was glad she'd be reporting to Sergeant Capretto. She'd worked with him once before—well, she'd been one of many, actually the whole women's force had been on uniform duty that night, so she couldn't expect that he'd remember. It was the night of the big sweep of Times Square. That was how long ago? Nearly a year, and if they were to repeat the raid tonight, they'd pick up mostly the same vagrants and hustlers and so on. Which made it seem useless, but if you took that attitude she reasoned, then there wasn't much point in being on the force at all.

The door of 8B was ajar. Norah rang anyway, hesitated, was about to walk in when it was pulled open all the way.

"Ah, Officer Mulcahaney, right?"

She was absurdly pleased. "Yes, sir."

"Out of uniform."

"I was off duty. I didn't think I should take the time—"

"Right. Come on in. What did you find?"

Norah was glad she'd done her job before coming up; nevertheless, she was having trouble with the clasp of the double-handled policewoman's handbag which was normally so manageable. Why should she suddenly be so clumsy? She reddened, stopped, tried again, brought out the handkerchief bundle. "Only three items, Sergeant. But one of them . . . of course, I couldn't really see too well by the streetlight. . . ."

The phone rang in the bedroom, and Joe held up his hand indicating that she should follow him. Everything had been dusted for prints, so there was no problem about handling the phone. He picked it up and listened silently, grimaced, and handed it over to Norah, nodding vigorously.

"Yes? Who is this, please? . . . Miss Smith. . . ."

The sergeant backed off, shaking his head.

Norah got it. "Sergeant Capretto isn't here just now, Miss Smith." She received an exaggerated sigh of relief from Joe. So now she could speak with assurance. "This is Officer Mulcahaney speaking. May I help you? . . . I'm sorry, I don't know where you can reach him at this time. He may have gone home, I really can't say. . . . Well, if it's urgent, I suppose . . ." She glanced toward the sergeant.

Raising his eyes heavenward, he sighed, and took a resigned step forward.

Norah was spurred to one last try. "If it's urgent, Miss Smith, shouldn't you give me the message? I'll try to contact him and have him call you, but in the meantime, we can be acting on your information." Norah had become very firm.

It produced results. She listened awhile. "That was four days ago? I see. . . . And will you give me that other number again, please?" Without fumbling and with the use of only one hand she opened her handbag, got out a small notebook, found a pencil, and made the notation. "Thank you, Miss Smith, thank you very much. We'll get on this right away. Oh, and Miss Smith, the sergeant will be notified, and I'm sure he'll want to thank you himself." She hung up.

"Well, thank you, Mulcahaney. Thanks a lot."

"It seems deceased complained to the telephone company about nuisance calls. They sent her the usual form, but she didn't follow through. The calls must have been more than a nuisance, though, because she contacted the company again and requested a new and unlisted number. The business representative said she was nearly hysterical, and the new number went into effect just four days ago. This is the old number." She tore the leaf she had written on out of her book and handed it to him.

Joe heaved one of his extra deep sighs. "You're right; I owe Miss Smith a call. Okay if I do it in the morning?"

Norah tried to hide her pleasure. "That's up to you, Sergeant."

But Joe's mind was back on the problem, which gave Norah a chance to look around—the first chance she'd had. The incongruity of the open window and the turned-down bed struck her right away. "Sergeant, two of the items in that bundle I handed you are a locket and a bracelet. It looks to me as though they were given to her by two different people."

Capretto untied the bundle and took a look. "You're right. The 'Clem' of the locket would obviously be Clement Emerson, her husband, who died recently in an automobile accident. The capital 'J' on the bracelet must be the initial of the giver and the small 'c.m.c.' could be a quotation or stand for a private phrase, who knows? Or the bracelet could have been a family keepsake."

"Ah, I don't think so, Sergeant. That locket is definitely old-fashioned, but the bracelet is modern." She joined him beside the lamp on the night table. "That design, I don't know a lot about jewelry, but notice the mesh base and the raised gold links, particularly the angularity of each bar. That kind of jewelry has only been on the market for the last ten years or so. Notice too the color of the gold—kind of reddish; that's eighteen karat. American artisans use fourteen karat. So that comes either from Europe or South America. I know because my brother Mike wanted to give his wife jewelry for their tenth wedding anniversary, and I went shopping for him. They're out in Indiana," she finished lamely.

"Fascinating, Mulcahaney, absolutely. What you're trying to say, tactfully, is that the bracelet was a gift from another man."

Norah nodded.

"Interesting, if true, but irrelevant."

"How can you know that?"

He was startled. Rookies, particularly female, didn't challenge sergeants. On the other hand, she did rate being filled in.

Norah listened with her full concentration. "The call could have been bad news. . . ."

Joe was pleased. He nodded. "And given the state of mind she was in—"

Norah frowned. "She was recovering."

"It wouldn't take much to make her slide back."

"And jump out the window?" Norah's square chin jutted out. She'd made up her mind.

Was it determination or stubbornness, Joe wondered. Then he spread his hands out, palms up, in the typically Italian gesture of his childhood. "All right, the bracelet will be traced."

"Yes, sir."

He decided to show her what she was overlooking. "The point is, Mulcahaney, that even if there was a boyfriend, we have to place him at the scene and the doorman says she had no visitors, not tonight or anytime."

"Somebody from inside the building maybe?"

*Oh, she's sharp, no doubt of it,* Joe thought. "What we need is a witness." He stared thoughtfully out toward the building across the street. He made his decision. "What's your name?"

"My name? You know. . . . Oh! Norah."

"Well, Norah, you'd better get over there and start ringing doorbells."

She'd already followed his glance. Now she was looking at him. "Me?"

"I've got a report to write. I don't know who else is available, but I suppose I could find—"

"Yes, sir!"

"Wait, wait. Hold it a minute. You just ask if anyone happened to be looking out the window tonight between eleven fifteen and eleven thirty. If so, whether they noticed if this window was open. That's all. *You let them tell you.* Get it?"

"Yes, Sergeant Capretto. Nowadays they give a course in interrogation at the academy."

"Is that so? And how long since you graduated?"

"A year."

"Then hopefully you remember some of it."

It took her several seconds before she could reply with a docile "Yes, sir." Then, almost in spite of herself, she added, "I'll exercise caution and avoid leading the witnesses, Sergeant."

Joe bit back a grin, nodding sternly in dismissal. He let her get away with it this time, only because he had other things to worry about. The report of the nuisance calls and the recentness of the change in the telephone number worried him. It could be coincidence, of course, but in cases of violent death coincidences should be regarded warily.

# Chapter 3

The water came to a roiling boil, and Joe Capretto removed the heating element. One thing he couldn't tolerate was the taste of stale coffee flavored with cardboard. If anything, the new plastic containers made it worse. So he carried his own electric coil, assured that whatever precinct he might be working out of there would be instant stashed in somebody's desk drawer and a sugar hoard in somebody else's. Why the two were never in the same drawer, he didn't stop to analyze. He'd found what he wanted and was now stirring the viscous combination when he caught sight of Norah Mulcahaney.

She didn't see him. The desk he was using was located behind a column. The whole precinct house had been scheduled for demolition—twelve years before. Meantime, girders had been installed and enclosed in plaster columns to support the sagging ceiling. The squad room was nearly empty; she didn't think anybody was watching, so she let her weariness and dejection show.

It was 4:30 a.m.

Capretto stuck his head around the column. "Mulcahaney! Over here."

She stiffened instantly and came over.

Joe'd been about to offer her coffee, then decided not to. "What took you so long?"

She blinked, then stared straight at him. "I stopped to type my report." Carefully she laid the neat pages in front of him. "And the carbons." She put those down too, a separate pile.

He took care not to show he was impressed. "That means you didn't get anywhere."

"Nobody saw anything."

"It was a long shot, you know." He glanced over the

papers. "Name of tenant, apartment number, telephone, and résumé of activity at relevant time. Concise. Good, Norah. Very good. Thanks."

"Thank you, Sergeant."

"It's a good report, but you forgot something. How do you expect to get credit if you don't put your name on it?"

"I thought it would go in with your stuff...."

He shook his head dolefully. "You'll never get ahead that way, Mulcahaney." He handed her his pen. "Okay, now go home and get some sleep." But she hesitated. "Well?"

"Is that all?"

"For now. Unless . . . you have a suggestion?" He was weary and running out of patience.

"I was thinking about those nuisance calls."

"And the fact that she'd only had the new number for four days," he finished for her. "It occurred to you that in all probability whoever knew the new number must have been someone Ruth Emerson trusted or she wouldn't have given it to him."

"Yes, Sergeant."

"And it seems like too much of a coincidence."

"That's it." She was eager now.

"On the other hand, *she* could have called *him*. Have you thought of that?"

It was evident she hadn't and didn't want to.

"Norah, are you getting personally involved in this case?"

She was genuinely surprised. "No, I don't think so. Why should I?"

"I don't know. It happens . . . and one never really knows why."

"I'm not."

"Good. So then let me give you a piece of advice." Grinning engagingly as he knew very well how to do he tried to make it easier for her. "Don't be stubborn about evidence." Before she could rear back to defend herself, he went on. "Don't get hung up on any one solution and try to bend the facts to fit."

"I didn't realize—"

"I'm only pointing out to you that there's sometimes an inclination to do that. Collect facts without any attempt to make them fit. Keep loose, mentally. One other thing: You may become morally certain how, why, and by whom a crime was committed, but the knowledge is useless without proof to back it up. In this particular case we don't *know* whether the call was to or from Mrs. Emerson. She could have been talking to . . . her broker who told her she'd just been wiped out in the market, or her doctor reporting that those X rays confirmed the worst, or any of a number—"

"Neither of those would be likely on a Sunday night."

"Don't be so finicky—those are examples. The point is that if we can't prove anybody was with her, then we have to accept that she jumped of her own accord."

"Because of the call."

"Yes, all right, because of the call!" He was getting testy. "The call was the cause. Okay. You're claiming it was intentionally so."

"Yes, I am. Otherwise, why didn't he call back when she dropped the receiver on him? Shouldn't he have been worried? Shouldn't he have tried to call back? When she didn't answer, shouldn't he have tried to contact a neighbor or even the police?"

"Murder by telephone." Joe Capretto stared straight at Norah. "How are you going to prove it?"

He wasn't a man one would be likely to remember, not, that is, if one brushed against him accidentally on the street, or edged by him on a subway, or sat next to him at the theater. A second look wouldn't mean much—he was depressingly average, middle-class, and "square." One would have to look very hard to penetrate the regular assembly-line face, stare deeply into the close-set eyes to catch the curiously unfocused look. And why would anyone trouble to do it?

Those who thought they knew him, those who worked with

him and associated with him daily would not have recognized him in the creature that sat on the bed, face mottled with rage, mouth drawn so tight it made the sinews in his neck stand out like the highlights of a medical chart, fists clenched, watching the telephone.

He'd made it a rule never to use his own phone, but the temptation was tremendous. He kept telling himself that it was useless since she'd left the receiver off the hook again, that it would have to wait till morning. He distracted himself by planning what he would say to her in the morning. He was too nervous to undress and go to bed properly. He'd stretch out for a few minutes till he calmed down.

He awoke at seven still in his clothes, rumpled and sweaty, his mouth foul with the taste of cigarettes, every nerve taut. His hand reached instinctively toward the phone, shaking. But he pulled back. *Stick it out,* he warned himself, *only a little longer.*

The room stank. God! he'd smoked too much. He never smoked at all except when he was nervous; it was bad for him. That was her fault, damn her. He threw open the window top and bottom to air the place, shook out the bedspread and replaced it. He stripped down, tossing the suit onto a chair, where it would be picked up for cleaning, and the discarded shirt and shorts into the hamper. In the shower he rubbed himself till his body tingled. He cut himself shaving, and the blood stained the fresh undershirt. Oh, damn her. Damn her.

By the time he was ready it was too late to go around to the Hampton Towers. Maybe he'd just put in a call from the drugstore downstairs. When he got there, somebody was already in the single booth. All right, he'd have a cup of coffee. A *Daily News* lay on the counter stool beside him. Generally he spurned tabloids, but today he'd been so preoccupied he'd forgotten to bring along the *Times* that was delivered daily. So he riffled through the trashy pages while he waited for the jerk in the phone booth to stop yakking and give somebody else a chance. The passage was so insignificant that if he weren't versed in scanning small notices, he would have missed it.

His first reaction was dismay. The man vacated the phone booth finally, and sliding off the stool, he instinctively started toward it. Then full and complete realization of her death made him back off violently.

"Watch out!"

He registered only that the woman he'd knocked into was a common, cheap, dyed blonde, and she was in his way.

"Say, listen! What do you think you're doing?" She was stunned, but she recovered quickly. "What are you—some kind of nut? Son of a bitch!" she yelled after him. "Did you see that?" she asked the sympathetic counterman. "He just shoved me aside. Never apologized or nothin'."

"Didn't pay for his coffee neither." The counterman added his own complaint. *"Yahch!"* he spit as he swept the counter clean and tipped the dregs of the coffee into the sink. "We got all kinds in this city. All kinds, believe me."

For the next few days he felt disoriented, lost. It had never lasted such a long time. People at the office were beginning to notice, to ask what was wrong. He resented their prying. The resentment was transferred to the dead woman, and from resentment he passed to anger. He fed the anger, then let it consume him. He came out of it spent and weak, but with a new understanding.

Norah got home at daybreak. She tiptoed cautiously through the apartment and considered it a good omen that she hadn't wakened her father. Quickly she undressed and slipped between the sheets as the first reddening light appeared in the sky. She was excited, restless, managed a few hours' sleep, and was up at eleven in the hopes of hearing from Sergeant Capretto. When no call came, she reported for her regular tour, barely able to suppress the tingle of excitement that still lingered, trying to act normal. Not that she expected immediate results from last night's events, but the sergeant had certainly indicated that she had done well and that her work would not go unnoticed. Maybe she'd be assigned to help trace the bracelet? Maybe....

Sergeant Capretto brought his report personally to the lieutenant so he could give a verbal rundown. There were things that couldn't be put on paper—hunches, misgivings. It was why Lieutenant James Felix encouraged these informal résumés. He believed in facts; he also believed in impressions. Now, as he listened, his high brows arched higher.

"So." He punctuated the end of the sergeant's account. Then he summed it up. "You aren't satisfied she jumped."

Capretto grimaced. "I don't believe she was pushed."

Jim Felix understood the dilemma; he was as sensitive and intuitive as any of his men, even at second hand. "If the problem is *why* she jumped, that's not our business."

Joe knew it too, still.... "Lieutenant, suppose I come running in here yelling 'Fire!' I tell you the stairs are blocked and the only way out is the window, and you jump. But there isn't any fire. I caused your death."

"Suppose you really believed there was a fire, then what?"

"Well, if there'd been smoke and maybe an alarm sounded, then my intent could be proved—either way."

"All right. Prove it."

"Yes, sir."

"Cap!" Felix called him back. "Clement Emerson died in an automobile crash. There'll be reports of the accident. About the bracelet—it's not likely to be a custom piece, so go on down to the wholesale district and see if you can find it in one of the catalogues. Once you've got a list of the retail outlets . . . well, you've got the initials on the bracelet, haven't you? You can just about handle the whole thing from your desk."

"Yes, sir."

"So it should all be wrapped up in—two days. Two days—right, Cap?"

Which was the lieutenant's way of telling him that was all the time he could be spared. Joe wasn't inclined to argue, to point out that possibly the bracelet hadn't been bought in New York or even in the United States. That would have involved wasting some of his allotted time. "Yes, Lieutenant."

He decided to consult the accident report first, only because it would be readily available. It meant a call upstate, of course, but Joe figured the lieutenant had sanctioned that. The report was read off to him, and it in turn led him to the Universal Kitchen Supplies Company and Charles Staff.

Staff was a big florid man with a bulbous nose to go with his high color and surprisingly a flat stomach negating both. He had white, bushy hair which he wore well clipped but with sideburns. His shirt was striped, the collar and cuffs white and extra-wide. He wore a fire red tie. He was turned on, but he was also a member of the Establishment. He was the sales manager. He'd heard about Ruth Emerson's death. He was shocked. He also had plenty of time to talk.

Clem Emerson was a great guy, Staff told the sergeant. Quiet, serious, nothing flashy, but he gave out with a kind of *sincere* quality. . . . get what I mean? He talked as if he really believed in the product. Now the customer senses that. Emerson's style was understated, but it worked. He got results. Yes, sir.

Toward the end, though . . . well, Emerson'd been slipping. At first he, Staff, had figured, you know, Emerson was having a run of bad luck. Happens to everybody. He was always quiet—Staff boomed on as though to emphasize his own energy—but there was something different in it at the end: Emerson was brooding. So Staff had pulled him aside and talked man to man with him, not to pry but to find out what was bugging old Clem so he could hold out a helping hand. Part of the job, you know, Sergeant. Besides, he really did want to help. But old Clem wouldn't admit anything was wrong, so what could Staff do? He had to drop it. Though by then he had a pretty good idea what it was all about anyway. Trouble at home. Usually is.

Staff passed a big hand back from his forehead to make sure his hair was in place.

It was one of the standard problems, the sales manager assured the sergeant. The men went on the road, and the women stayed behind and they got bored. What could you expect? Especially when there were no children and the woman was as good-looking as Ruth Emerson.

Joe remembered what Ruth Emerson had looked like on the sidewalk.

Naturally, Staff went on, he didn't know for a fact that that was what was bothering old Clem, but he'd be willing to give odds. Certainly he wasn't suggesting that Emerson went over the edge of that road purposely. God, no! He did think, though, that the road, treacherous at best, was on that particular day, afternoon, wet, slippery; the visibility was bad, and Clem Emerson was too preoccupied to take the proper care. If the sergeant wanted to know, Staff thought that was what had been bugging Ruth Emerson. But don't take his word, talk to the other salesmen, talk to the secretaries. Go ahead.

So Joe did just that and got confirmation right down the line: Mrs. E. had been playing around; Emerson knew or suspected; Mrs. E. felt responsible for his death. Nobody could supply the name of the alleged boyfriend.

The next step was the bracelet marked with the "J." Following the lieutenant's suggested procedure, Joe discovered that it was indeed of standard design and manufacture. He got a list of the retail outlets. From those he in turn got a list of the purchasers. There were, surprisingly, not that many whose first initial was "J," and even fewer who had ordered the bracelet monogrammed.

By the following morning, on the sixth try, Joe had located the customer who had ordered the particular monogram he was after. His name was Julio Valdes and his address 20

Sutton Place South. Doing a little homework before the interview, Joe discovered that Valdes was an Argentinian working for an American firm and that the job called for him to commute back and forth—without the company of Señora Valdes.

Valdes was on the still hopeful side of thirty-five, elegant, handsome, consciously charming without being offensive, and he didn't bother to pretend surprise at the sergeant's visit. He readily admitted the affair and appeared engagingly frank about his qualms regarding Clement Emerson's death.

He had broken off with Ruth immediately after, he told Capretto. Well, he qualified with a shrug that expressed apology, regret, and self-justification all at once, almost immediately. A certain tact, delicacy, was called for, wouldn't you agree? He had written a note of sympathy, then waited perhaps . . . two days . . . after the funeral before telephoning to suggest that under the circumstances it might be best if they did not see each other for a while. He told her he was returning to Buenos Aires. A small prevarication—to make it easier for both of them, no? She understood. She was very reasonable. Valdes sighed, again, and it was all regret. That was one thing, one of the many things, he had appreciated about Ruth—no temperament, no hysteria. She was so practical, so . . . American. Ah . . . it was a pity, a great pity; they had suited each other. Of course, after the way the husband died, well, it could never be the same again, no? You understand? He appealed to the sergeant as another man of the world. Even if they could have brought themselves to resume, people would always hint, imply that somehow in some way the accident had not been an accident. People always preferred to think the worst—so much more titillating, no?

Valdes claimed to have been genuinely shocked to hear of Ruth Emerson's suicide, but he could not believe their breakup was the cause. No, he had not called her the night of June 1, nor had she called him. The last time he'd spoken to

Ruth was on the occasion he had just recounted—he consulted his desk calendar and made it May 7.

Joe had one more question.

Ah, no! Julio Valdes' smile was tenderly reminiscent; no, surely he did not mind divulging what the initials of the inscription on the bracelet he'd given to Ruth meant. They stood for the phrase *con mucho cariño*, with great affection, which he had felt for her and with which he would always remember her.

Joe walked thoughtfully back to his car. A feeling of guilt over her husband's death had predisposed Ruth Emerson to suicide. It didn't explain the phone's being off the hook . . . or maybe it did. Sure. Everybody in Clement Emerson's office guessed at his wife's infidelity. Maybe somebody knew. Maybe that somebody was threatening to tell. The final threat combined with her own inner guilt had been too much.

It made sense. The lieutenant would buy it. Joe bought it himself.

Each day that passed Norah expected to be called in to the director's office. While she waited, she went about her regular duties energetically, if with divided attention. The days passed more and more slowly. She began to chafe at the waste of those powers of observation and reasoning which she willingly admitted she hadn't known she possessed till the duty in the Emerson case. A week went by. Another week. The disappointment was hard. She went over every word she and the sergeant had exchanged. There could be no doubt that he had been satisfied with her performance . . . maybe even liked her. She brushed that aside. The point was she couldn't expect any help from him, shouldn't have ever—he was under no obligation to speak for her. . . .

When the mayor had called in experts to do a study of the department it had resulted in a big shake-up. Responsibilities were shuffled, jobs melded, some eliminated, and the duties of policewomen had not escaped scrutiny. More than three hundred women had been assigned to individual precincts where they reported directly to the commanding officer—lieutenant or captain. Norah had remained in the general pool at Centre Street. She'd been new on the force; it hadn't mattered to her one way or the other. Now she felt that she'd been passed over. A new class would be graduating, and there would be new postings. She watched for it eagerly, telling herself that it was certain she would be transferred this time.

Spring became summer; the city tensed for it. There were too many people with nothing to do. The heat frayed the nerves of the calmest and best intentioned. The heat sapped Norah's patience.

The list went up, and her name was not on it.

She stood rooted in front of the bulletin board, the hot flush of disappointment and shame on her face. Abruptly, she turned and pushed through the crowd of women behind her, head down so they wouldn't see how close she was to tears. She could feel May Cuddahay looking at her. May had been on the force as long as anyone could remember. A comfortable women, not well educated, she seemed satisfied in her slot. She took on herself the duty of den mother to the new recruits, maybe as a consolation for not having been promoted in all those years. She was always ready with sympathy. Norah held back the tears, arranged her face, and walked steadily to the stairs that led to the locker room. Cuddahay was right behind her. At least she had the tact not to say anything.

Norah changed into uniform as quickly as she could. She kept from even glancing in Cuddahay's direction—a glance would be enough to encourage her pity. Finished, Norah slammed her locker with unnecessary force and started to leave. Then she hesitated. May Cuddahay had been around a long time; she knew all the ins and outs. It wouldn't hurt just to ask.

"How do you get assigned to Homicide?"

The question came out abruptly, much more baldly than

she'd intended, and now she tensed for the reply. If Cuddahay laughed or made any kind of crack, she'd never speak to her again.

But Officer Cuddahay could only gape. "You?" she managed finally.

"Why not?" Norah countered instantly, feeling herself burn.

The older woman shrugged. "I don't even know if they have women on Homicide. I don't think so."

But once started, Norah persisted. "Detective then? How do you make detective?"

"Well, you know . . ." May Cuddahay was embarrassed. She searched for a tactful way, but there wasn't any. "You ought to get assigned to a precinct for a start."

"Is that the only way?"

"The director could recommend you. . . ." That was another blunder because obviously if the director thought well enough of Norah, she would have been on the day's list. Not wanting to hurt the kid, May hurried on. "The commissioner could do it. He can do anything." Now she was really embarrassed. She hadn't meant to imply that it would take the commissioner's intercession for Norah to get her wish.

Pat Mulcahaney carried the beer back to his easy chair in front of the television. "Who scored the run?"

"Huh? Oh, I don't know. I didn't notice," Norah replied.

"Why bother to sit there if you're not going to watch? Do you even know who's pitching?"

"Oh, Dad, of course I know who's pitching. I took my eyes off the screen for a minute and somebody scored, so I missed it, that's all. I'm tired."

"And cranky and hard to get along with."

"I'm sorry."

"You need to get out of the house, have some fun. It's not right for a young girl to be sitting home watching TV with her father."

"I like sitting here with you."

Mulcahaney sighed heavily. "What's eating you, Norah? What's wrong?"

"The new precinct postings went up today. My name wasn't on the list." She just blurted it out.

"Ah . . . well, sweetheart, you've only been on the force a year."

"Most of the other women who graduated with me were on it."

"But not all?"

"No, not all."

"There you are then. You'll be on it next time."

"Oh, Dad, you just don't understand!" She got up and walked away from the television. "I'd been expecting . . . I was so sure. . . ."

"Try to have a little patience."

"Dad, some of the women who graduated with me were on it last year already. Some of this year's rookies are on it!"

Though he regretted she'd ever joined the force, Pat Mulcahaney didn't like seeing his child hurt. He held out his hand to her, and when she placed hers in it, he kissed it. "All right then, have you asked yourself why? Have you been trying to run the department? The director has been there a while longer than you, and she might not appreciate that you know better than she does."

She snatched her hand away. "I might have known you'd make fun of me."

"I'm not, sweetheart." He reached forward and turned off the set just as the Mets were coming to bat, but for once Patrick Mulcahaney wasn't interested. "You're used to giving orders here at home, and me and the boys were used to taking them from you. But it's different outside."

"I . . . I don't mean to be bossy."

"Of course you don't. It's our fault. We thought it was cute—a little girl telling off three grown men. We spoiled you." He saw the tears come to her eyes and felt his own brimming. It would be good if she would come to him and they could cry together. But she was too proud. He had been too at her age. He watched sadly as she turned away from him toward her own room, heard the door close softly, and knew she would do her crying alone.

He switched the television back on and sat down. He sat there till well into the seventh inning, and he had no idea of the score. By the time he realized the phone was ringing and got up it had cut off in the middle of a peal, meaning Norah had picked up the extension in her own room.

He strained to hear but couldn't. Mulcahaney wasn't prepared for his daughter's transformation as she flung herself into the living room, wearing fresh lipstick and carrying her heavy handbag.

"What kind of duty is it this time?" Her reluctance was all the answer he needed. "It's no job for a woman—searching dead bodies."

"Suppose I were a nurse?"

"You're not a nurse," he countered with that same querulousness of which he'd accused Norah. "Anyhow, why does it always have to be you."

"I don't suppose it would have been me if Sergeant Capretto hadn't asked for me. Dad, he particularly asked for *me*."

# Chapter 4

It was an urban renewal neighborhood, but the house Norah wanted had been passed over. She spotted it by the usual contingent of police vehicles parked at the curb in front: a couple of radio prowl cars, the ambulance, assorted shabby sedans, and unmistakably, Sergeant Capretto's maroon Mustang—testimony to his single, living-at-home status. Recently installed neon streetlights flooded the block. People hung out windows on both sides of the road. The crowd on the sidewalk as varied ethnically as economically were subdued, sharing one thing at least this hot July night—awe in the presence of death.

Even as she made her way through the throng, Norah was uncomfortably aware of the curious stares. She didn't return them, simply showed her identification to the patrolman on guard and was directed toward the basement apartment, its small arched doorway tucked under the high front stoop. The first thing she noticed even before entering was that both the windows at ground level were shattered, but that the glass of only one lay on the sidewalk.

She stepped directly into the bedroom. It was a low, cramped room, untidy, as though nothing had ever been put into drawers. Maybe housekeeping just seemed hopeless under the conditions. The ceiling and floor sagged; the rough plastered walls showed unexpected bulges, sure indications of serious leakage. The furniture was secondhand and mismatched. The double bed hugged the wall on one side to make room for a sagging mahogany bookcase obviously homemade and a metal office desk. And the books were everywhere, shabby volumes with faded lettering and broken spines. Norah's nose twitched uneasily. She coughed. Once again she turned toward the broken windows, understanding now why one had been broken from the outside and the other from the inside. She steeled herself for what she was sure would be in the other room.

Nominally the kitchen, it was both parlor and dining room as well. A big room—and in its center sat the dead girl. Once Norah saw her, she forgot her smart deduction. Oh, Lord! she thought. Oh, blessed Mary!

"You all right, young lady?"

Norah opened her eyes and realized that she was swaying. Vaguely she registered who it was that had spoken to her but still couldn't stop staring at the young woman sprawled in the shabby armchair in front of the open oven, at the dark head lolling limply to one side, at the thick book in her hands, at her legs splayed wide, at the enormous mound of her abdomen.

"Oh, dear Lord," she moaned aloud. "Dear Lord!" she repeated and made the sign of the cross quickly. Then, a little more composed, she was able to shift her gaze. Yes, it really was Dr. Asa Osterman, and behind him were two police officers with emergency oxygen equipment. There must be more to it than a straight suicide to bring the medical examiner himself to the scene. Of course there was, she instantly reminded herself—in killing herself, the young woman had also murdered the child in her womb.

"If you're going to be sick, there's a toilet back of that door," Osterman barked. He was relieved to see Norah stiffen.

"Thank you, but I'm not going to be sick."

"Then get on with it. We haven't got all night," the little man growled. "This is a rush job—for a change."

Norah nodded and stepped forward. The pregnant girl had been young and pretty, too, probably before the gas discolored and bloated her. Her hair was dark, cut crisply short and feathered around the once-small, peaked face. Her entire build was slight, almost elfin, and it was this delicacy that made the distention of the abdomen seem even more enormous than it actually was, almost abnormal.

Involuntarily Norah turned toward the doctor, the question in her eyes.

"If she'd waited another day, we might have been able to deliver the child," he grunted, but behind their plain glasses his lashless eyes were as full of pity as Norah's. "That's an unofficial guess," he added testily.

So, gently, Norah removed the old Bible from the small, work-roughened hands, noting with a new pang the ragged fingernails childishly bitten to the quick. She slipped off the simple gold wedding band easily enough. There was no other jewelry, not even an engagement ring. The search was quickly finished, for besides the abdominal support, the dead girl wore only a slip, robe, and out-of-shape backless slippers.

"The sergeant's waiting for you." Asa Osterman's terrier bark brought her back. "You go out the way you came to the street and up the front to the first apartment. That is if you're finished, Officer Mulcahaney."

She was surprised and gratified that he knew her name; the sergeant must have mentioned it. "Yes, I'm through, Doctor. Sorry to hold you up."

"*I'm* not the one who's in the hurry. You tell your sergeant he won't get the results any quicker by calling me every half hour either. You tell him that every time I have to answer that phone we're both wasting time. Make sure you tell him."

"Yes, Doctor." Norah stifled her smile, but Asa Osterman had already dismissed her and was yipping out a set of orders to his crew.

On her way through to the street Norah paused for one more look around the dilapidated bedroom-study. Probably the husband was the one still in school. Where was he? Upstairs with the sergeant or still attending class? Surely, someone had thought to notify him? There was a phone on the metal desk and beside it a scratch pad. The top sheet was covered with doodles, all the whorls decorating a single number. Norah's eyes widened. She riffled through a couple of stacks of papers and quickly found what she was looking for. She took the double sheet and ran out into the street and up the high steps to the main building entrance.

"Come on in, Norah," Cap called out to her from the open apartment doorway.

He was having coffee, seated comfortably at a round table in the middle of an old-fashioned, overfurnished parlor. Opposite him was a gray-haired, hook-nosed, sinewy old woman of about sixty dressed completely in black. The only adornment she wore was a pair of small pearl earrings that pierced her earlobes, probably inserted the day of her baptism and not removed since. Obviously she had been in full spate of talk when Norah appeared. Obviously, too, she was annoyed at the interruption.

"Excuse me, Mrs. Zabrina." Capretto's courtesy was splendid as he rolled out her name with the rough "Z" and trilled "R" and full Italian resonance of the vowels. "This is Officer Mulcahaney, Mrs. Zabrina. Want some coffee, Norah?"

Norah started to say no. "It would help," she admitted instead. "Oh, please don't disturb yourself, Mrs. Zabrina. I'll get it, if that's all right?"

She was rewarded by an approving nod from the sergeant and a slight easing of Mrs. Zabrina's resentment.

"Mrs. Zabrina is the neighbor who called us about Mrs. Neumann," Capretto explained genially as though it were a social event. "It seems Victoria Neumann had an appointment with her obstetrician this morning which was canceled because the doctor was making a delivery. Late this afternoon when his nurse called to make another appointment, she got no answer from the Neumann apartment. She kept calling, and by about seven thirty she became concerned— Mrs. Neumann being so near term. She got in touch with Mrs. Zabrina here and asked her to check to see that everything was all right. Mrs. Zabrina knocked and couldn't get any answer either. She inquired around, but nobody had seen

Mrs. Neumann all day. So Mrs. Zabrina went for the super. He services about a dozen of these buildings. When she couldn't locate him, she called the police."

Norah had filled her cup from the two pots on the stove—one of coffee, the other of boiled-over milk—and brought it back to the table. "You did the right thing, Mrs. Zabrina. You're a good neighbor. It's nice to know there are still people who aren't afraid to be good neighbors."

The old lady was gratified. Her selfconscious nod was followed by a sigh of real regret, and tears rose easily to her eyes. Though they were facile, Norah saw that they were nonetheless honest and that the old lady had cried before. "It was too late to save her!" Mrs. Zabrina moaned. "Maybe if I donn'a wait for the police . . . if I break the window myself . . . maybe something could be done for the *bambino*. . . ."

"The doctor says not," Norah reassured her.

"Ah. . . ." She looked searchingly at Norah. Believing her, she wiped the fresh tears away with her bare hand, snuffled a couple of times, then abruptly pushed forward a plate on which there was a high glossy cake with only one slice cut out of it. "Please, have some *panetone*. Is very good . . ." she hesitated over what to call Norah. "Go on, meess . . . it goes good with the coffee."

"Thank you, it looks delicious." Norah noticed the remains of the one missing slice on the sergeant's plate.

Lucia Zabrina beamed, then settled back importantly. "Now, what was I telling? Ah . . . so, Sergente Capretto." She rolled out his name as he had hers in the mother tongue. "Vittoria was a girl of such spirit, friendly, always cheerful. Everybody in the block—they love her. Then she get pregnant and is not the same. Well, it happens like that sometime with the first child. A woman becomes . . . how shall I say? . . . moody, dissatisfied. We make the allowances." She said it with all the indulgence of a woman who had herself borne many children. "Also, she has to give up her job. That means with her husband away there is little money. But the real bad thing is to be alone. Is hard for a woman without her man at such a time."

"Where is Mr. Neumann?"

This time the interruption excited Mrs. Zabrina. She caught her breath, glanced at the sergeant, and was quick to speak before he could. "He was drafted, the young man, into the Army. In the beginning, Vittoria visit him in the camp, but then he is sent to Vietnam. The poor young man. He is killed t'ree weeks ago."

"Oh, no!"

"Ah! You can imagine!" Mrs. Zabrina threw up her hands, reacting to Norah's reaction. "His body is shipped back, and we all go to the funeral. Ah, she was so brave, the little one. For myself, I think is not natural to hold so much sorrow inside. Not good. Is shock, I tell to myself, and when the shock is gone . . . ah, then will come the bad part. And you see, I was right. *Ai, ai, ai!*"

Norah glanced quickly at Capretto. She was sure he had already asked, but she couldn't resist asking herself. "How long ago was the funeral?"

"Eleven days—exactly."

"And she's been alone down there all that time? No relatives to stay with her. No friends?"

"She send her family away. She not want them. Her friends . . . we are all her friends, and we all try to help her. I bring the hot soup; she will not open the door. I come back; she shout to me to leave her alone." Mrs. Zabrina spread out her arms, then let them drop. *"Ah, Santa Maria Vergine, prega per noi!"* She began to moan, rocking back and forth.

"Mrs. Zabrina!" Norah leaned toward her. "Let me get *you* some coffee. It will do you good."

"Thank you, child, thank you."

Norah filled the cup, placed it before the tough and kind old lady, and sat down again. "You said Victoria Neumann gave up her job when she got pregnant . . ."

"Not right away, no, later, when she is too big . . . you understand?"

"Was her husband already in the Army then?"

"*Certo, certo.* He has been many months in Vietnam. Did I not say it?"

"I have all that information." Capretto decided he'd left Norah on her own long enough. He got up.

Norah took the cue, retrieved her handbag and the double sheet she'd put beside it when she poured the coffee. Should she mention it now? Capretto caught her eye and shook his head slightly. So Norah added her good-byes and compliments to his as Mrs. Zabrina with gushing friendliness escorted them both to the door.

"I see you spotted the telephone number," Capretto remarked as soon as the door shut on them and they were alone in the hallway. "And recognized it and found the annoyance sheet, too."

He was always ahead of her. "I did some checking of my own. On my own time," she added hastily.

"Did I say anything? You're too sensitive, Mulcahaney."

Her father said she wasn't sensitive enough. You can't win. "I called the telephone company and said I was getting nuisance calls and what could they do about it. They sent me the same sheet; but I said I wanted to discuss it with somebody, and they gave me that same number."

"Did you call it?"

"Uh-huh. I got advice. They told me not to show fear or hysteria, in fact, not to talk at all, that talking only fed his neurosis. The best thing I could do, they said, was simply hang up. I asked them if they couldn't trace the calls, only because I'm sure that's what Ruth Emerson must have asked, and of course, they explained how I'd have to keep him on the line. Not a nice prospect for someone who's harassed and frightened."

"It's the routine advice and it was given to Vicky Neumann."

"You've already checked?"

"Your opinion of me is showing, Mulcahaney."

"I didn't mean . . . it's just that . . . well, you only got here, you really haven't had the time . . . I'm sorry," she finished lamely.

"Mrs. Neumann didn't want her number changed."

"Why not?"

"Could be a number of reasons—the simplest that she didn't want to go to the trouble of notifying her friends. Or that as she'd already made up her mind to die, the calls were just a minor harassment."

"Then why bother to contact the telephone company at all?"

"You've got a point."

"Having survived the shock of her husband's death and the ordeal of the funeral, what could have happened that was so much worse that she killed herself?"

"You heard Mrs. Zabrina . . . the reaction, the full realization. . . ."

"But to destroy the baby along with herself?"

That bothered Joe too, more than he cared to admit. "Maybe she thought the world too ugly and cruel to bring a child into. Maybe she killed herself as an act of mercy to the child. Hell, I don't know what these kids are thinking these days."

"She wasn't a kid."

"Maybe she just didn't want the baby."

"Then why didn't she get rid of it right away? It just seems too much of a coincidence for both Mrs. Emerson and Mrs. Neumann to have been receiving anonymous telephone calls."

"Have you any idea how many women in this city are harassed like that?"

"There must be a lot or the telephone company wouldn't print up those sheets. I only know that two of those women are dead."

He tested her some more. "Suppose I tell you that we've uncovered a motive for Ruth Emerson's death that would tie in with that last call she got? And that there was a suicide note in the desk of Victoria Neumann's bedroom? Then what?"

It slowed her down, but she wasn't ready to give up. "Then why did you get Dr. Osterman down here? Why are you so anxious for the autopsy results?" Before he could answer, she rushed on. "Dr. Osterman said to tell you he'd let you know as soon as he has something and not to be calling him every half hour. What do you expect him to find?"

"I don't expect anything. I just want to make sure that nobody knocked Victoria Neumann on the head or put a pillow over her mouth before artistically arranging her in front of that oven."

Norah gaped. "But you said there was a suicide note."

"I said there was a note. I didn't say Victoria Neumann wrote it." He opened the door to the street and let her precede him down the steps.

"Sergeant?"

"Don't you think you know me well enough to call me Joe?"

"Joe . . . suppose, he, whoever he is, calls again tonight? I could wait and answer. . . ."

"And get his name and address?"

She pressed her lips together till she could speak calmly. "If he knows she's dead, he won't call."

"Uh-huh . . ." Cap nodded several times. "And if he doesn't know she's dead and he calls, that means there's no connection."

"That's logical."

Joe thought about it. "I suppose it's worth a try."

# Chapter 5

Lieutenant Felix gazed out the window behind his desk at the familiar slice of courtyard and sipped the hot coffee Cap had fixed and brought in with him. Amazing, Jim Felix thought, what an accurate indication of the weather you could get from the way the sun hit that brick wall and the tint of that narrow border of sky visible above the smoke stacks. It was 7:25 a.m., and already the morning redness had sharpened into an eye-hurting glare. The heat wave was nine days old, and the whole department had turned to weather forecasting—and the whole department would be wincing at the prospect of another hot one.

Felix sighed. No use moaning over what you couldn't help. He swung his swivel chair around and put the thick white crockery mug down. "You make good coffee, Cap." He pulled up to the desk and rested his elbows on it.

"So. The note was typewritten. There was a typewriter in the room, and the type matches. So that leaves us right where we were before. Asa reports no indication of a blow that might have rendered Victoria Neumann unconscious before the gas was turned on, no trace of any drug either."

"What's bugging me, Lieutenant," Joe explained, "is that it's the second time. Two apparent suicides, both preceded by anonymous telephone calls, both women recent widows. The odds against it—"

"We could feed it into a computer, and I'm sure we'd get astronomical figures," Felix agreed. "It still wouldn't prove anything, not even that the calls were made by the same man."

That was one Joe hadn't even considered! He should have. He frowned. It made what he had to tell next harder. He did want Norah to get credit for her willingness. "Officer Mulcahaney volunteered to wait in Mrs. Neumann's place in case of another call."

"She did, eh? With your permission naturally."

"Yes, sir."

"Kind of a long shot."

"Worth trying, sir."

"Hm." Felix made a temple of his fingertips and tapped them back and forth against each other. "I think the Mulcahaney girl is getting under your skin, Cap."

Joe winced; it was exactly the reaction he'd anticipated. "No, sir, believe me. I like Norah, sure; she's good-looking, intelligent, and very intuitive. . . ." At the instant frown, Joe knew he'd goofed, used the wrong word anyway. The lieutenant had married a young actress who was nothing if not intuitive herself; it had landed her in plenty of trouble, that intuitiveness, and the lieutenant too in getting her out. Not that Maggie Felix meddled and not that she didn't turn out to be right in the end—it was the in between that was so rough on everybody. Joe tried again. "What I mean is that Officer Mulcahaney seems to have an aptitude for investigative work. She reasons logically, for a woman," he amended, not wanting to overdo it.

Felix grinned. "That's quite a tribute. It'll be the end of an era when you get hitched."

"Hold it, Lieutenant! My God! I like her, but I like all the girls." He shrugged. "Anyhow, she doesn't like me."

"I can't believe it!" Felix gasped in mock horror. "She must be a very unusual girl. Just as well maybe. If she's as good as you say, we want to keep her on the force awhile." He became serious again. "Look, Cap, I'll admit the way the coincidences are piling up bothers me. On the other hand, there's absolutely no indication either of these women was murdered. They might have been harassed to the point of taking their own lives. I think we could say so in the Emerson case. So. Now you'll check into Victoria Neumann's background."

"Yes, sir." Joe got up and removed the coffee mugs. "I was wondering . . . Officer Mulcahaney is familiar with both cases. If I could borrow her for a few days. . . ."

"She's under another command."

Joe opened his mouth and shut it just in time to avoid doing what he had cautioned Norah against—arguing a superior's decision. Felix could request a temporary transfer; they both knew it. So he had his reasons for refusing. Joe turned at the door. "More coffee, Lieutenant?"

Felix shook his head "Tell you what, I'll alert the center and all precincts to refer complaints about nuisance calls to you."

"Yes, sir. Thanks, Lieutenant." Inwardly, Joe groaned. Good God!

After Cap left, Jim Felix swiveled around to face the blank courtyard wall again. Undoubtedly there were strong similarities in these two deaths, and he was more concerned about them than he had cared to let the sergeant know. He hoped that Cap would find as much to reinforce the suicide theory in Victoria Neumann's death as he had in that of Ruth Emerson. He had no doubt that he would—only a vague, uneasy, damned . . . suspicion. With the unsettled condition of the city and the summer heat as goads, even a rumor of a psychotic killer could put the city on the edge of panic.

The aura of Vicky Neumann's death and that of her unborn child pervaded the small basement apartment. As the curious neighbors returned to their own homes, as the street sounds faded, as everyone else went to sleep, Norah sat beside the telephone waiting. She was too keyed up to be bored, but the hours did drag. Well, she had asked for the duty, begged for it. Suppose the call came—what would it be like? Norah had never been the victim of that kind of harassment, and she dreaded it. But she was sure it wouldn't come because she was sure that the caller was responsible for Vicky Neumann's death.

She hadn't realized she'd dozed till she was awakened by

the ringing. She sat bolt upright in the chair and stared at the telephone . . . instantly alert and frightened. What had she let herself in for?

"Norah?"

It was only Joe.

"Sorry to disappoint you, Mulcahaney."

"Oh, no, that's all right." She was ashamed to be so relieved.

"Nothing, I suppose?"

"No, nothing."

"Well, we didn't really expect there would be, did we?" He paused. "The lieutenant says go home, get some sleep, and report for your regular duty."

"Oh. Yes."

So that was that. She couldn't reasonably have expected to be kept on the case. She reminded herself that when a policewoman had been needed, Joe had asked for her. Maybe he would again. Just the same, she couldn't shake the nagging disappointment. She collected her things, and it wasn't till she stepped out into the street that she realized it was morning. Somehow she managed to get into the apartment and to bed without disturbing her father.

She awoke sluggishly to bright sunshine and the sound of voices in the living room. Not feeling up to making small talk with one of her father's cronies, she dressed slowly in the hope that by the time she was ready he would be gone. But he wasn't, so there was nothing for it but to come out and make the best of it.

"Good morning, sweetheart."

Well now, she knew her father and if he was going to beam on her like that instead of quizzing her about how late she'd got in and why, he had a good reason. One look at the visitor, and she knew what it was.

"Meet Henry Sorlein, sweetheart. My daughter, Norah, Henry. Henry's looking to rent an apartment in the building."

Sorlein had risen to his feet and was smiling at her.

But she was too annoyed to be polite. "I didn't know we had any vacant apartments here."

"The vacancy was next door, but by the time Henry got there it was gone. The super suggested he try here. We met in the lobby." Her father explained eagerly, much too eagerly. "Henry's in a sublet now, but he has to get out at the end of the month. Henry's an accountant," he finished lamely.

"I'm sorry if I disturbed your rest, Miss Mulcahaney. Your father told me you're a policewoman and that you were on late duty last night."

He was ordinary enough, Norah thought. On the short side, somewhat stocky, in his mid-thirties. He wore a dark-brown summer suit and a brown striped tie—he looked like an accountant. His eyes were small and deeply set, but he had a good strong jaw and a shy smile. She could tell that he was sensitive to the situation. The shared embarrassment served to create a bond between them. Norah smiled back. "You didn't disturb me. I had to get up pretty soon anyway; I'm due back on duty in a couple of hours."

"I'd better be going then."

"Oh, don't go yet," her father blurted and then looked abashed as they both turned to him.

"I'm on my lunch hour," Sorlein apologized.

Patrick Mulcahaney hobbled along with him to the door. "I can inquire for vacancies around the neighborhood for you, Henry, if you'd like."

"That's very kind of you, sir. I really appreciate it." He looked back over the old man's shoulder. "It was nice meeting you, Miss Mulcahaney."

A minute later Norah fixed her father with a stern look. "Was he really looking for an apartment?"

"Of course. What do you think—I picked him up on the street?" He was righteously indignant.

"I wouldn't put it past you. You did ask him up here to meet me, though, didn't you?"

"I was being neighborly."

"Oh, Dad!" She shook her head.

Relieved that she wasn't angry, he added, "He seemed too nice to pass up."

"You're hopeless." She ended up laughing, as she always did.

Mulcahaney laughed with her.

Capretto decided Victoria Neumann's obstetrician was as good a witness to start with as any he could find.

Office hours were just ending, and "Doctor" had already gone to "Hospital" for rounds, but "Nurse" (obviously British) would gladly assist in any way if "Sergeant" would be good enough to wait for a few minutes while she dispatched the last of the patients. Joe took a chair and, while flipping the pages of the inevitable *National Geographic*, listened and watched too as she reassured and encouraged a woman who was certainly well past the childbearing age. He got the impression that "Doctor" was all cool efficiency and scientific dispatch while "Nurse" provided the old-fashioned soothing sympathy. A canny combination.

Maude Bright had improbably red hair; but her blue eyes were genuine, and so was the concern in her flaccid round face. Her uniform was starched and spotless, and she was rigidly corseted into it. Joe sensed she tolerated it for duty hours, but that once inside her front door the casing would most probably be shed and she would spread in all directions.

Nurse Bright waved the sergeant to the patient's chair beside her desk and lit up. She took a long drag, exhaling slowly. "I'm constantly preaching to my girls not to smoke; if they could see me! It's about Vicky Neumann, isn't it?"

Joe nodded.

"I thought so. I've been worried, I don't know why. Everything was going well. She'd finally settled down, had even begun to take some pleasure in having the baby, and yet. . . . When I couldn't get through to her yesterday afternoon, well, I knew she took in work at home—typing, research, so on—so that the chances of her being out for any length of time, except for marketing or a breath of air, were slim. Even the necessary excursions would be down to a minimum—she wasn't getting around too easily anymore." Maude Bright paused, looking abashed. "I don't want to imply I had any kind of premonition, though I do believe if one is close to a person one can sense. . . . Doctor laughs at me." She tossed her flaming red hair. "If I hadn't been able to get through to Mrs. Zabrina, I would have gone over myself."

"You were afraid she might harm herself?"

"Oh, no, nothing like that. It was because she was alone. Accidents can happen. A woman so near term is ungainly, she can fall, faint. . . . To start with, Vicky's physical conformation made it a difficult pregnancy; she was anemic, plus the fact that her state of mind was not the best. One would not have known how much she really wanted that baby."

"Is that so?"

"Of course many women are wild to conceive; then when they do and they discover what it's like, they're sorry. They resent the sickness, discomfort, particularly losing their looks, and of course the restrictions. They get impatient. Vicky's being alone made it that much more difficult."

"Her husband's death surely affected her state of mind."

"Well"—Nurse Bright weighed her words carefully—"in a way it seemed to quiet her. I suppose she realized then that the baby was all she had left of him. I suppose then she was really glad they'd made the effort."

"I don't follow."

Nurse Bright lit another cigarette and decided to loosen the belt of her uniform. "You see they hadn't planned on a family quite so soon. The idea was to wait another year at least till Tom, that was her husband, had finished his law studies and got himself situated. But then he was drafted. They reasoned that by the time he got out, resumed his studies . . . well, she didn't want to wait that long. So she made a point of going down to visit him at the camp. Quite a distance, too, North Carolina, I believe she said. I gather she made three trips before it took."

"But you said her state of mind was bad from the beginning. Shouldn't she have been elated?"

"I imagine her feelings were mixed, not having wanted the baby that soon and under those circumstances."

"You would say then that her husband's death actually strengthened Mrs. Neumann's wish to bear the child."

"Definitely."

"Did Mrs. Neumann mention to you that she was being bothered by anonymous telephone calls?"

Maude Bright's entire person expressed her shock and concern. "No. What kind of calls?"

"We have no idea."

"Do you think the calls could have been what upset her to the point— No," she decided, answering her own question. "No. In spite of everything, Vicky was a sensible, rational person. She wouldn't let some crank drive her to take her own life."

"She is dead, Miss Bright, and so is the baby. There is no indication that it was anything but suicide."

But there was now an indication, one he hadn't suggested to Nurse Bright, one he would follow up and that might just bring him back to her and the doctor for confirmation. Joe didn't think the lieutenant would authorize an overseas call, but some of the boys in Tom Neumann's outfit would surely have been shipped back by now, the wounded. The Army would have a list; the Army had lots of lists.

Corporal Richard Bosley wounded in the shelling of headquarters base on the Ninth Infantry Division at Dong Tam forty miles south of Saigon, now in the intensive care unit of the Veterans Hospital at Bethesda seemed to fill the bill.

The lieutenant said, "All right. Go and see him."

Joe got a jolt walking through that ward, not at seeing so many wounded or at the degrees of their injuries and their patience, though in each instance it was phenomenal, but at their youth! Children! Just children. Which meant he was getting old, and that was a jolt—of another kind. He ought to settle down, start a family of his own, make some girl happy. At least he should start thinking about it.

Corporal Bosley had his own problems, bad ones. His right leg had been blown off in the explosion of an ammunition storage pad. What was left of the thigh was infected. The surgeons were worried. He was heavily and continuously sedated. Joe had to wait till most of the last dose wore off; then he had to compete with the returning pain for the corporal's attention.

Yeah, sure, Bosley had known Tom Neumann. Bosley's once-round, once-young face showed the first twinges of a new attack. He tensed at what he knew was coming. He and Neumann weren't buddies or nothin'; Neumann was a drag, one of those guys that never gripe, got their minds on bigger things! He was like in another world, looking to the day he'd be getting out, just going through the motions meantime. You know what? That guy actually had his wife sending him law books so he could study in the bunker! Feature that!

"I guess he figured his wife wouldn't be going back to work after the baby, so he was in a hurry to get his degree," Joe commented.

It elicited no response from Bosley.

Capretto tried again. "Was Neumann rooting for a boy or a girl?"

Bosley twitched in irritation. How in hell should he know?

"Didn't Neumann tell you his wife was expecting?"

"Like hell! He never said a word. God! Where's that nurse? Where's that needle? You know what?" Bosley writhed. "You know what? There are plenty of times, plenty, when I figure Neumann was one of the lucky ones."

The nurse came and gave him the injection.

Bosley slumped in relief.

"Listen," he told Capretto, "if his wife was expecting, Neumann wouldn't have kept it no secret, he'd'a taken an ad in the *Stars and Stripes*. That is, if the poor slob had'a known about it."

\*\*\*

Thomas L. Neumann's Army record naturally listed his blood type. It was not compatible with the baby's. Thomas Neumann could not have been its father. A solid, irrefutable fact. Did it matter who the father was? Maybe. Tom Neumann's death hadn't hit his wife as hard as it should. Maybe because it was a relief.

In its way this was as simple and ordinary and sordid a story as Ruth Emerson's: a cheating wife, a complacent husband, a lover—this one balking at his responsibility. Maybe Vicky Neumann had thought her baby's father would marry her when Tom Neumann died. His refusal would have been enough for her to kill herself and his child.

That left the phone calls out of it, but maybe they'd never been in.

Joe was picking all this out on the typewriter when his phone rang and the desk officer announced a Mrs. Arabella Broome.

# Chapter 6

She was tall and slim with a pale pinched face, and her amber eyes were frightened. Silver hair was brushed back from a high brow, falling like loose strands of silk, cut bluntly but unevenly just at the chinline—a home job. She wore a navy blue linen suit, loose and ill-fitting. Its skirt reached just below the knee, not long enough to be maxi, Joe, who prided himself on his appreciation of women's fashion, thought, just out of style. She clutched a pair of white cotton gloves that were mangled but still clean at the fingers, indicating she had not had them on. She was surely under twenty.

She hesitated at the threshold of the squad room looking around uncertainly. Even when Joe rose to identify himself and started toward her, she still hesitated. He had the feeling she might turn and run, so he moved a little more quickly and smiled as reassuringly as he could. Whether his manner had anything to do with it he couldn't tell, but she made her decision and, clearing a loose strand of hair from her face, marched forward.

Close to, in the direct light, Joe could see deep blue circles under her eyes, like bruises on that fresh skin, and indicative of more than just one sleepless night. The worry lines across her brow were there to stay. He pulled out a chair for her. "Sit down, Mrs. Broome."

"I suppose you know what this is about?" Her voice, high and breathy, restored the image of extreme youth and vulnerability.

"I'd appreciate hearing the details from you."

She worked her lips nervously, taking time to choose her words. "I think someone's trying to make me go out of my mind."

It wasn't what he had expected at all. "Why?"

"I don't know why." She replied flatly, careful to avoid emotion.

"You don't seem frightened, Mrs. Broome."

"Oh, I am. Yes, I'm frightened." She let it show momentarily. "But I'm angry, too. Also, I'm confused. I don't know this man, I don't know what he has against me. Well, that's not exactly right. I know what he accuses me of, but it's not true. And anyhow, why should he pick on me?"

"I think you'd better start from the beginning."

"You mean with the phone calls?"

"If that really is the beginning."

He didn't know how she'd react to that. By implication she'd already denied that the calls had anything to do with her past. Maybe they didn't, but if she'd talk about it, he might find out.

Arabella Broome's slim frame trembled with her own doubt. Obviously, she'd agonized over that point. She squirmed in the chair. Her face twisted till she was as wrinkled as an old woman. "I want you to understand it wasn't easy for me to come here, Sergeant. It's a long time since I've had friendly contact with . . . the police. Buddy hated the *fuzz*, and what Buddy thought or felt was good enough for me. Besides, once you've been turned on, it's not so easy to turn yourself off again. Especially when you're alone. Not easy at all." She paused.

Evading the question though she was, she was still revealing a great deal. It brought Joe's alertness to its sharpest.

"Of course it all goes back to Buddy, to meeting him, falling in love with him. If not for Buddy, I wouldn't be here now. But I don't blame him. I don't blame my parents either. They tried to stop me; why wouldn't they? According to their standards, he was shiftless and dirty and irresponsible—everything they'd been taught to condemn. He had no job.

He played his guitar in coffeehouses, theater lobbies, or parks or on street corners if he couldn't get in anywhere else. He passed the hat, and that's what he lived on. I think the reason I was attracted to him was that he seemed so free, you know? I mean, he had no obligations; he didn't have to be anywhere at any particular time. He didn't have to account for what he did or who he did it with. He went where he wanted, and if he got bored, he just moved on. He didn't owe anybody but himself, see? The only debt he had was to himself. I'm not preaching, Sergeant, I'm just telling it like it was . . . or like I thought it was at the time.

"He never offered to marry me; all he said was if I wanted, I could go with him. And I wanted. Afterward we got married. He knew I was uncomfortable without that piece of paper; he knew I was still hung up on the religion bit. He did it to please me is all. It didn't tie him to me any more than before. With or without the license he would have cut out any time our harmony stopped. I knew that, and I was grateful for the gesture. I was glad to be able to write my parents and be able to tell them we were married. I never got an answer, though. I kept checking general delivery in every town, but we were moving fast. . . . The letter probably got lost. . . .

"Up to then I didn't turn on. I didn't condemn it, don't think that; I believe everybody should travel his own road, but . . . the truth is the whole thing scared me. What I mean, I like to keep control, you know? Besides, I didn't need acid or pot or anything to understand Buddy. He didn't try to sell me either. Still, when he went on a trip, I felt left out. So when he married me, well, I wanted to show I was grateful." She looked pleading and defiant at the same time.

"I understand."

"Do you?" She seemed surprised, but she didn't dwell on it. "It wasn't so bad at the beginning, but I didn't like it much either. I suppose I never got over being frightened, I never really let go, I stayed uptight, so I never really had a good trip. But I realized how much it meant to Buddy, and I didn't tell him it was no good for me. I don't know if it would have made any difference if I had told him, but then he was pretty much turned on most of the time. Anyhow, I guess you know what happened. He died. Three weeks ago. In Chicago."

So here it was—death of young husband, widow alone in the world . . . Joe waited.

"Maybe if I hadn't tried so hard to be like Buddy. . . . You see, I was high when he died. He was right there beside me, and I didn't know. . . . Maybe I could have saved him."

The guilt! Joe shuddered. Here was the guilt, too—the pattern repeated for the third time. It could no longer be ignored. He swore to himself it would not be.

Arabella Broome pulled herself together. "I didn't know his people; he never mentioned them, but I knew that originally he came from New York. So I brought him back. I got myself a room, had a telephone installed, and put announcements in the papers. I hoped his family would see the announcements. But nobody got in touch with me. For all I know Broome wasn't even his real name."

"You did all you could." She didn't answer. "He died three weeks ago you said, and you came right to New York?"

"Yes."

"Surely if his people had seen your notices, they would have contacted you right away. Why didn't you go home?"

Again her amber eyes met his. "I wanted to pull myself together first." She invited him to examine her drawn, sad, old face—submitted it as evidence. "I thought I'd get a job, put on a little weight . . . I guess I'm a square after all, like Mom and Dad. . . ." She wasn't going to be able to hold the tears back much longer.

So that explained the baggy suit and the haircut and the cheap cotton gloves. "I'm sure they want you back, even though you are a little thin and a little tired. Why deny your mother the joy of fattening you up?" Joe smiled at her.

"Not yet. I have to be sure . . . that I'm all right."

He knew what she meant, and his heart went out to her.

Then, he became very practical. "Well, let's get back to the phone calls then. When did they start?"

"I buried Buddy on Tuesday, so probably it was that Friday or Saturday...."

"You mean you don't remember?"

"Oh, I remember. I remember every single one, but I'm not sure . . . which were real. It's not that I was high. The day Buddy died, that was the end of it for me. I was finished, through, believe it. But I guess it was still in my blood, a residue like they warn you, and it would just swamp me, all at once, without any warning—it would just suck me under. I didn't know whether I was asleep or having a waking nightmare. Those first few days after the funeral I thought maybe the calls were part of a trip. I'd pick up the phone, but I wasn't sure it had really rung. I'd hear the voice, but after I'd hung up, the voice still kept on. It was all around me. It came out of the walls, it echoed like in a cave. And the foul things . . . the foul things . . . the foul things...."

Silently, Joe put his handkerchief into her hand. He waited till she'd recovered. "Want some coffee?"

She shook her head. "It wasn't like that between Buddy and me, not like he said." She swallowed. "Then one morning, a week ago, when I was too sick to be high, when I knew, just knew, that I was in the real world, the phone rang again. . . . I answered, and I recognized that same voice, and I knew that the calls had been for real all right, all of them from the very beginning. I asked him who he was and what he wanted. I told him he was sicker than me, and I hung up on him.

"He called right back, mad, and warned me never to hang up on him again. I told him he didn't scare me, that if he didn't leave me alone, I'd go to the police. And you know what? He laughed, yes, he did; he said if I went, I'd have to tell everything about Buddy and me and then it would be in all the papers. I wanted to run away and hide. I thought of moving, even changing my name."

"You could simply have changed the telephone number."

"I thought of it."

"Then why didn't you?"

She took a deep breath and, sitting very still, bit out each word precisely. "Because . . . I . . . want . . . him . . . caught."

"So you came to us."

"Not right away. Like I said, I'd got used to ducking the—the police. I'd got leery. So I tried to figure it out on my own. I figured he couldn't be a stranger. What I mean is, it just didn't seem possible that a stranger would stick a pin in the phone book and come up with any number and then pour out so much hate. . . . Besides, he knew about us, about Buddy and me, how we lived, how we moved around, how we'd waited before marrying. He knew about Buddy's past and how he died. It couldn't all be guesses. So I decided to try to find out who he was.

"But I think he knew what I was up to and teased me along. He'd let me ask questions and give sort of vague answers and then hang up only to call back a few minutes later. Sometimes he'd call six or seven times a day; other days he skipped completely. I'd get nervous waiting; it was almost worse not hearing. Last night I was fixing myself something to eat, around seven it was, he called and announced he wanted to make sure I'd stay home and mourn for Buddy, so he'd be checking me every hour or so. He warned me to be there. Well, I knew what that would be like and I just couldn't take it. I left the phone off the hook. But I was so scared I couldn't sleep anyway. By six a.m. I was so rattled I put it back. He rang right away.

"He was vicious, vicious. The things he said . . . about why I left the phone off the hook, about what I was doing while it was off . . . I can't repeat . . . I don't want to remember. . . ." First she covered her eyes; then her hand moved down to her mouth as though to choke back the words. "He said if I ever did it again, he'd punish me in a way I'd never forget."

"He actually threatened physical harm?"

"He didn't say what he was going to do."

"In your conversations were you able to find out anything

at all about him? Where he lives, even the general area, what he does for a living, anything?"

"No."

Capretto heaved one of his energetic sighs. "It won't be easy to identify him. Your husband having been an entertainer and the two of you moving around so much, it could be someone you've never even met but who's observed you both and has fixed his resentments and delusions on the two of you."

"I was hoping you could trace the call."

"That's not as easy as people think. It takes time, from twenty to thirty minutes, and all that while you'd have to keep him talking. Even after the trace you have to occupy him so that the officers can get to the location. Can you do that?"

She stretched her thin neck. "I *will* do it."

Well, thought Joe, whoever *he* was, whatever his contact with Buddy and Arabella Broome had been, if any, whatever he was up to, this time he'd picked the wrong victim. He looked hard at the girl.

"Okay, Mrs. Broome, wait right here."

Lieutenant Felix's green eyes were thoughtful. He rocked back and forth in the swivel chair.

"Let's assume the calls are real and not induced by residual effects of the drug she'd been taking or by her sense of guilt at having taken them, plus the shock of her husband's death and the fear of her parents' condemnation. We still have only her word that he actually threatened her. This kind of deviation is an escape from reality. The kicks come from the subject's reaction, from the fear and revulsion she expresses. Even if he wanted to, he couldn't bring himself to actually lay a hand on her."

"Usually." Joe said.

"It's what the psychiatrists tell us. My feeling is that a fever unchecked is bound to rise. Particularly in this instance where the girl is not reacting satisfactorily. She's fighting back and adding to his frustration, instead of easing it. Under the circumstances he might progress to physical assault." Felix paused. "You've explained to Mrs. Broome what's involved? And she's willing?"

"Yes, sir."

"All right. Set it up. And, Cap, as long as we're doing it, let's do it right. Set up for a voice print. In addition to the phone company's tap, get a direct line to us from Mrs. Broome's apartment . . . well, you know the drill."

"Yes, Lieutenant."

"One more thing—you mentioned that on a couple of occasions he called her right through the night. Now that indicates to me that he's making some of those calls from his own home."

Joe's dark eyes flashed. "So we should wait to make the trace till real late. It'll be easier then, too, the lines won't be so busy. But . . . suppose he doesn't make any late calls for a while?"

"Those calls in the quiet of the night, waking her up from her sleep . . . those are the ones he's hooked on. He needs them like an addict needs his fix. We'll wait."

Still Joe hesitated. "Lieutenant? It could be a long wait, and then when it happens, it'll happen fast. Will Mrs. Broome be able to handle both phones and keep him talking and remember the recording device? It's an awful lot . . ."

"Oh, I'll assign someone to be with her. But not you. I think it's a job for a woman."

Joe grinned. "Yes, sir, I think so, too."


Norah had to cancel a date with Henry Sorlein. They'd seen a lot of each other since the morning her father had brought Henry up from the lobby to meet her. She was aware that in his quiet, methodical way Henry was conducting an assiduous courtship. Now thinking back over the dinners and movies and the quiet evenings in front of the television, she realized that they'd settled into a pattern: weekends, Tuesdays, and Thursdays. She didn't mind—in view of Henry's reticence, it was an indication of his seriousness. It was the first time she'd had to break the schedule, though, and she couldn't help wondering how he'd react. This was Thursday; would he ask her for Friday or wait till Saturday?

Henry was disappointed, but understanding. He suggested that as long as she would be working, perhaps he could come over and watch TV with her father.

Norah hadn't expected that. She was miffed. "Sometimes I think Henry is as satisfied to sit home with you as to be with me, that all he really wants is companionship."

Instantly Patrick Mulcahaney defended Henry. "He lost both parents when he was just a kid, and he has no family of his own at all. You ought to be glad he's family-minded."

"I am, naturally."

"He's only too willing to take you out; you're the one who's always saying, 'Let's stay home' and turning it into a threesome. The trouble with you is you don't know what you want."

"I suppose so." Norah sighed. "If he were only a little more aggressive. . . ."

"There you are! You said Artie Webster was too aggressive."

"I know, but Henry treats me like . . . like—"

"Like the woman he wants to marry!" Her father finished for her. "That's what he treats you like. Henry's a good worker. He's steady. He'll look after you."

"Is that all there is to marriage, Dad, security?"

"Oh, sweetheart, of course not, and I want you to have it all. You just don't understand Henry."

There was a dangerous darkening of her clear gray eyes. "And you do?"

"That's right, I do. Henry respects you. So that means hands off till you're married."

"Then why hasn't he asked me to marry him?"

"Maybe he hasn't had a chance."

"Is that why you turn out the lights and scoot into your own room every night when you hear us come in?"

The natural ruddiness of his face deepened; then he began to chuckle. "Ah, well, I'll not deny I want to give the boy a push. And you too, love, you too." The brogue he took good care of never losing, considering it a political asset, now broadened beguilingly. "You're somewhat unapproachable you know, darlin'. If you could unbend a little...."

"You want me to seduce him, is that it?"

"I'll not have you speakin' like that!" His anger died immediately. "It's the job that makes you say such things. Let Henry see the soft, tender girl I know you are."

"If he doesn't see it, if he doesn't know it, what's he bothering with me for at all?"

That cry, all Irish yearning, cheered Mulcahaney. It meant that in spite of contact with the ugly and the evil, with the predators and their prey, Norah was beginning to realize that the only sanity in this world catapulting to its own destruction, the only solace, was in the love between a man and a woman, in their mutual trust and respect. "Well, if he doesn't he's a bigger fool than I thought!" Mulcahaney barked and kissed her resoundingly.

"Oh, Dad, it's just that I'm not sure, don't you see? I like Henry; of course, I do. He's a little dull, but he's considerate and thoughtful . . . I suppose I could do a lot worse."

"Give yourself time, sweetheart. Get to know Henry better. Maybe Henry senses your feelings; maybe that's why he hasn't spoken yet. Maybe he doesn't want to risk being turned down."

"Maybe." Norah smiled. "But don't you keep him here till all hours waiting for me. I don't know how long the duty will be; it could be all night."

For once Mulcahaney didn't fuss. He didn't even ask what kind of duty it was that might keep her out all night. He had more important things on his mind. He kissed her again and sent her off. Just as well he and Henry would be alone tonight. Give him a chance to have a little talk with the lad, put some spunk into him. After all, with himself and the boys as examples you couldn't expect Norah to respect a Milquetoast.

Arabella Broome had found herself an efficiency apartment in a remodeled brownstone in the Chelsea section of the twenties. The furniture was cheap Danish modern. The kitchen was at one end of the single long room partitioned off by a venetian blind that could be raised or lowered. The bathroom had originally been a closet. But it was all snug and neat. Somehow Norah Mulcahaney couldn't credit the scrubbed floors, the clear windows, and polished, dust-free surfaces to any efforts of the landlord. Nor could she help comparing it to Vicky Neumann's place.

"You're a good housekeeper," she told Arabella Broome.

Joe Capretto could tell right away when he introduced them that the two young women took to each other. They had, he thought, the same qualities: courage, determination —fighters, both of them.

"I haven't anything else to do." The slender blonde disclaimed Norah's praise, but it was evident she was pleased by it.

"Is there a back entrance?" Cap asked.

"No, Sergeant."

"Too bad. I'd just as soon Officer Mulcahaney weren't seen coming in each night."

"You think he's watching?"

"Who knows?"

"I won't be in uniform," Norah pointed out.

"Hmm. Well, we'll have to risk it."

Norah kept on the problem. "Suppose Mrs. Broome were to leave the building before I came in? He'd hardly be likely to connect the two of us then."

Instantly Arabella Broome added to the scheme. "I usually do go down for a paper around six."

Norah was eager. "I could wait till she goes, then enter, and wait in an upstairs hall till she comes back."

"I'll have an extra key made and you can come right in."

The two smiled spontaneously at each other.

Definitely they were alike, Joe thought, intelligent, resourceful, and (he fervently hoped) level-headed under pressure. He remained carefully noncommittal. "Okay, I guess it'll work for a couple of nights anyway. Let's hope that's all it takes."

So he left them, but in spite of their instant attraction, there now rose a constraint between the two young women. Norah had never been so aware of her own blessings. She was afraid that any comment or inquiry about the other's life might sound patronizing or worse—as though she were condemning it. Arabella had fixed spaghetti for their supper. Norah had eaten before coming, but she was afraid to say so in case it would seem she was snubbing Arabella's hospitality. She also knew that the girl had very little money and that if she ate, she'd be literally taking the food out of the other's mouth. She decided that letting Arabella keep her pride was more important. Norah ate.

Arabella Broome would have liked to talk to Norah about her job, about how she'd decided to join the force, about what it was like being a policewoman, but she didn't want to appear to pry. She hadn't talked to another woman of her own kind—and she sensed that Norah was her kind—for months. She would have enjoyed talking to Norah about home, about her hopes of going back, but she didn't want to appear to be asking for pity. Or even worse—for financial help.

And there was another presence there with them—the silent but constraining pair of telephones. Arabella's regular phone rested on the table beside the studio couch; the new one had been installed on the bathroom wall so that the door could be closed and there'd be no chance of Norah's voice being heard on the first line. The eyes of both women kept straying to the phones, and each fought back her own anxiety. Arabella Broome now eagerly awaited the ring she used to dread, fighting the fear that maybe after all the calls had never happened at all, that the whole dreadful sequence had been an hallucination. The ugly reality was easier to bear than the unlimited, untold horrors of her own mind permanently disjointed. Oh, please, God, let the phone ring!

Norah, waiting, fought to still the doubts about her own competence. Would she be able to deal with the situation? It seemed simple enough: Arabella would pick up the receiver and turn on the recorder; Norah would then alert the officer manning the police line from her wall phone in the bathroom. What could go wrong? Any thought of her own aggrandizement was gone; all Norah wanted now was to help this girl in her trouble.

But there was no resolution of uncertainty for either of them that night.

The next night they followed the new procedure—Arabella going down to the corner for her paper, Norah entering, then Arabella returning.

"Anything during the day?" Norah wanted to know first thing.

"No, but he's skipped before, sometimes a couple of days," the blonde explained anxiously.

"Sure," Norah agreed. "Well, it's my turn to cook tonight." They had argued about taking turns, but not about the menu. It was obvious Arabella Broome needed good red meat, yet Norah hadn't wanted to be ostentatious. Seeing the way the girl eyed the bag of groceries Norah was glad she hadn't got the steak.

"You shouldn't have . . . you're doing enough for me as it is."

"That's my job."

"There's nothing in the job that says how nice you have to be. . . ."

"For heaven's sake, you're going to make *me* bawl."

The ringing of a phone paralyzed them both.

"It's mine. It's all right, it's mine." Norah rushed for the closet-bathroom to answer. The conversation was brief. "Just checking the line," she reported.

Norah cooked; they ate; they washed up; they read the papers. The time dragged.

"Why don't you go to bed?" Norah suggested. "You didn't get any sleep last night. No point in both of us staying up."

So Arabella made up the couch and took off her clothes while Norah crammed a chair into the bathroom and pulled the door to so that her light would not disturb the other girl or show in the street. She opened her book. She read without knowing what the words meant. Outside, the life sounds abated. Peering through her crack, she could see that the lights in the neighboring buildings had gone out.

The night passed silently.

Norah finished her book and looked at her watch—ten to four. She put out the bathroom light and pushed the door open quietly. The darkness was thinning; she could make out shapes in the room, and Arabella seemed to be sleeping. Soon it would be dawn, and another night would have gone by without his calling. Would he call tomorrow? Or did he suspect the trap? Had he been watching the house from some vantage and seen through their device? Maybe they should vary it tomorrow? She'd talk to Joe. She got up, stepped out of the bathroom, raised her arms, stretching her cramped body, yawned. . . .

The shrill peal was like a jab in the small of her back. She jerked forward, dropped her arms. . . .

At the first sound the girl on the couch moaned, at the second she sat up, reaching for the receiver.

"No, wait!" Norah's voice was a harsh whisper. "Take your time; he'll expect that you've been asleep—he'll keep ringing." She went to her wall phone. "Stand by, I think the call we want is coming through." She nodded, and Arabella picked up her receiver and switched on the recorder.

"Hello?" Her voice was low, as tremulous as ever, but her eyes brightened as she nodded vigorously to Norah.

"This is it," Norah told the operator. As soon as the call was traced, the location would be transmitted by radio to the sergeant who was waiting. Once she had initiated the sequence there was now nothing more for Norah to do than stand by with moral support for Arabella Broome.

The blonde looked sick; she was holding the receiver inches from her ear as though the instrument were contaminated. All at once her hold on it tightened, and she clamped it to her ear. "No! No! Wait!" she looked at Norah in panic.

"Have you got that location yet?" Norah whispered urgently into her phone.

"Please, wait. . . ." Arabella tried to hold him. "I have something to tell you." She paused.

She was about to go on when she heard a click and then silence. What had happened? Had they been cut off? Oh, no, please God, no. Would he call back? Should she hang up so that he could call back? She hesitated. . . .

Then a new voice—feminine, nasal, bland, recorded. "Deposit ten cents for the next five minutes, please."

Oh, God, they were going to lose him because of a damned mechanical device! Nobody had thought of the time limit on calls from a pay telephone. So now a mindless computer was going to wreck all the careful planning.

Then she heard a jingle, coins dropping into the slot—one, two, three; evidently the interruption had acted as a goad. "Now you listen, Arabella—" It was his sharp, by now familiar, hiss, and for once she was thankful to hear it.

Norah saw the girl wince and involuntarily hold the receiver away again. Then with an effort she put it back to her ear. "No, you're the one who's sick; you're very, very sick. I feel sorry for you."

The garbled sounds of indignation reached Norah across the room.

"All right then, if you're not sick, then you must have a reason for doing this, and I know what it is." Again she paused, stretching it out.

Norah had no idea what she was up to, but she admired Arabella's courage and resourcefulness.

"Since I don't know you, since I haven't willingly done you any harm, then you hate me because of Buddy."

The ugly, high-pitched laugh filled the silent, semidark room. Both girls shuddered; then the operator spoke to Norah. "We've got the location. The sergeant is on his way. You're to try to keep the subject on the line till he gets there."

"That's right, isn't it? I've hit it, haven't I?" Arabella persisting sensed that she had his attention and her confidence grew. This once she was on the offensive. "You knew Buddy. You must have known him before he met me. You must have been friendly with him. How friendly? . . . No, no, I'm not accusing Buddy. I *know* he didn't do anything wrong or even think it. But you, it's in your mind, it always has been . . ." The new spate of viciousness with which he responded was evidently too much. She appealed to Norah. "I can't, I just can't . . ."

Norah rushed to her and took the receiver from her. She was in time to hear the last few words distorted by rage. "You filthy, foul-minded, fornicating bitch. I know why you're trying to smear me. I know what you're trying to do. You're trying to get this call traced! You almost had me fooled, almost. . . . Don't think you'll get away with it. You'll hear from me again."

There was a clatter as though he'd dropped the receiver; the line remained open. Norah thrust it back at Arabella.

"Hello? Hello?" Arabella groaned. "He's gone."

Norah tried. "Hello? Hello?" She sighed. "No use." The two girls looked at each other blankly. Then the receiver in Norah's hand started to squawk. "Yes?" she asked eagerly.

"Norah! This is Joe. He's not here."

"He was on the line only a minute ago. He can't have gone far."

"He wouldn't need to. You know where this booth is located? On the corner of Sixth and Eighth. The heart of the Village."

"But at this hour. . . ."

"At this hour the coffeehouses and the joints are just

letting out. The street is jumping with weirdos. How do we pick one out of the crowd?"

"Oh." She tried to cover her disappointment. "What next?"

"Report," Joe grunted laconically. "See you at the office."

Norah hung up slowly. "The sergeant says not to worry." She hoped Arabella would not know it was a lie. She started to collect her things, avoiding the other girl's face while she got ready for fear of betraying the truth. The situation had deteriorated. Now that the caller knew that Arabella had actually gone to the police and that his calls were being traced, he'd keep them very short. If he called at all. Their chances had decreased—to put it optimistically.

"If there's any change, I'll call you on the police line. Otherwise, same arrangements for tonight. Your turn to cook." Norah managed a smile.

Arabella Broome nodded, but she wasn't able to smile back.

Jim Felix was pacing—a sure sign of agitation. "He's too damned careful!"

"Like he knows the ropes," Joe agreed.

"That's it. That's it exactly."

Norah watched and listened, diffident at this her first meeting with superiors. She swallowed, then decided that as she was included it was in order to volunteer an opinion. "Maybe he's already on the list of known offenders."

The lieutenant turned to look at her as though he'd forgotten her presence. "He could be," Jim replied quietly. "We could check it out and we wouldn't come up with anything beyond another list of those that were out on the streets at four this morning. We couldn't prove anything by that. Don't feel too bad, Norah; it wasn't a total loss. We may not have apprehended him, but I'll lay odds we've frightened him off. I don't think he'll bother Mrs. Broome again."

"Then . . . then he'll start on somebody else?"

"Probably, after a while, after he's got over the scare. There's nothing we can do about it."

Norah was shocked as much at the lieutenant's resignation as at the situation itself. "He told her she'd be hearing from him."

"What else could he say?"

"He was angry," Norah went on. "He was furious. She practically accused him of being a homosexual. I think the fact that she had the nerve to do it is what alerted him to the possibility of the call's being traced. She's never really stood up to him before. It drove him wild. I took the phone at that point, and I can tell you. He said he'd make her pay."

"Bluff." Joe dismissed it.

"I heard him, and *he meant it*." Norah insisted, ignoring Cap's warning shake of the head.

Jim Felix remained patient. "As you say you heard him and he was nearly hysterical with rage and frustration. But he did drop the phone quickly enough, didn't he?"

"Of course. He didn't want to be caught."

"So. You've said it. If he was wary before, he'll be doubly wary now. You know that if he calls at all, he'll keep it short—we don't have a prayer of making another trace."

Well, she'd feared that, of course. Norah bit her lip. "I'm not to go to Mrs. Broome's tonight?"

"You're to report back for your regular assignments."

"Yes, sir." She got up. Somehow she hadn't expected it to end this way. She started for the door, but she just couldn't go without one more try. "Lieutenant?"

"What is it, Norah?"

"Well, sir, everything you said is perfectly logical and rational. . . ."

"Thank you."

Joe raised his eyes toward the ceiling and groaned.

"That's what's the matter with it."

*Oh, no!* Joe thought. *Oh, no!* He wondered if there were any way to stop her.

"I mean I reasoned that myself. Anybody would."

Cap cast a horrified glance at the lieutenant, but Felix seemed interested. Cap could hardly believe it.

Norah went on earnestly. "This man is anything but normal or logical or rational: He's a maniac. And he's cunning. You both agreed he's been the route before—look at the way he chose one of the few areas in the city in which he wouldn't be noticed even at four in the morning, or maybe particularly at four in the morning, to make his call. So . . . wouldn't he figure that you'd expect him either to quit completely or at least lie low for a while?"

Felix passed a long bony hand over his long bony jaw. "What is it you want us to do, Mulcahaney?"

If she stopped to so much as catch her breath, her courage would be gone. "I think if he's going to do anything he'll do it fast. Tonight, Lieutenant. Please, could we have the stake-out one more night?"

That Tuesday evening at five thirty Norah Mulcahaney, wearing a flowered summer dress and carrying a raincoat over her arm, emerged from the subway at Twenty-third Street. She walked briskly down the two blocks, then turned west, slowing her pace. From the corner she should be able to spot Arabella coming down the front steps of the converted brownstone and crossing to the stationer's. Showers were predicted to relieve the heat, but it wasn't the preshower humidity that made Norah sweat. Her stomach was a hard knot. She shouldn't have spoken as she did in the lieutenant's office. She'd hardly needed Joe's black looks to tell her she'd been out of line. But the lieutenant hadn't been angry; in fact, he must have thought her reasoning accurate or he wouldn't have agreed to this one more try. Oh, dear Lord, make it work tonight! Make him call, and let us catch him. It wasn't that Norah cared about being proved right, about the commendation, even the possible promotion—not anymore. All she wanted now was to remove the fear from Arabella Broome's life. Maybe the lieutenant was right and she'd never be bothered again, but she couldn't know that for sure. Norah wanted to rid her once and for all of the spasm of terror each time the telephone rang.

Ah, there she was! No. Norah squinted at the blonde halfway down the block. She'd come out of the building next to Arabella's and anyway she was plumper and walked with a verve and self-confidence Arabella sadly lacked. Norah looked at her watch. She was late. She watched the door of Arabella's house. No one came out; no one went in.

By now Norah was almost at the front steps. She couldn't walk by and then come back; she'd have to go in. She climbed slowly to the fourth floor. Maybe Arabella had been a little early tonight? In that case, having seen Norah from the newsdealer's window she'd be returning any minute? Norah kept turning, and listening for the sound of the downstairs door. Or maybe Arabella was late. . . . Norah listened for sounds from above. The apartment house seemed unnaturally still.

If Arabella had changed her mind about the plan, if there'd been new developments, she would have called Norah at home—she had the number.

By the time she reached the fourth floor Norah was in panic. She rang the bell. She rang again and again, all the while looking over into the stairwell, expecting to see the blond girl on her way up. Then she remembered her key.

She pushed the door open only partially. It was enough. She could see it all from where she stood.

Arabella Broome had not left the apartment since Norah had been there. She lay sprawled across the unmade bed, her head dangling over the edge, white throat arched up, long, silky blond hair touching the floor, pale eyes wide and staring.

Lieutenant Felix had said the caller would never bother Arabella Broome again. He wouldn't need to. Norah began to cry.

# Chapter 7

Lieutenant James Felix came himself. Norah made her report, then moved to a corner. Felix asked her if she was all right, she nodded, and he left her alone. Joe Capretto cast a worried look at her every now and then but said nothing. The lab men came, the DA's men, Dr. Osterman—the room filled up; she was forgotten.

"I'll estimate the time of death as between ten a.m. and noon," the medical examiner growled. "I might make that a little more exact after I've examined the stomach contents. I assume you can see for yourself she was strangled. Put up quite a fight for her weight." Osterman stared at the splayed limbs, the disordered nightgown, tumbled sheets, and overturned furniture. "She died hard."

Joe indicated the door. "Bolt drawn, lock intact."

"So. She let him in." Felix brooded. "See if you can find anybody in the building who heard anything or saw anything."

"Yes, sir."

Joe Capretto didn't have far to go—Arabella Broome's neighbors were huddled at the far end of the hall. Unfortunately, they all were working people and had been at their jobs at the time of the attack. The super and his wife didn't live in the building. They were there in the early morning for the regular garbage removal and a light cleaning of the halls. Heavy washing and polishing were done once a week, Mondays. They seemed anxious to justify their absence. They had other buildings to take care of; they couldn't be everywhere at once; they followed a schedule; it wasn't their fault. Joe thanked them and without much hope continued on down the stairs and out to the street. The usual crowd milled in front. Maybe one of them had noticed a stranger in the block? All the answer he got was a shaking of heads—some sympathetic, some antagonistic, all regretful because each would have liked the importance of giving evidence.

"Nobody noticed anyone at all going in or out of this building between ten and twelve?" he persisted. "No deliverymen, laundrymen, repair people?" He tried to jog their recollections.

"There was a repairman, mister. I didden think you meant him." A thin, hawk-faced, sharp-eyed boy in his middle teens spoke up.

"What's your name, son?"

The boy pulled back, instinctively wary. "Ted."

Joe didn't press him for his last name, not yet. "I meant anybody at all that went into this building, Ted."

"What you talkin' about, man?" Another boy, stolid, big-shouldered, bully-chested, challenged Ted. "Didden nobody go in there!"

"Did too! I'm talkin' about the guy you clipped in the back with the wild t'row."

"Dat wasn't no wild t'row! And I didden hit nobody. The dumb guy walked into it. It wuz his own dumb fault. You tryin' to make trouble fer me, or what?"

Joe intervened. "Around what time would that have been, Ted?"

"How would I know that, mister?"

"How do you know he was a repairman?"

"Becuz he had on a uniform and he carried a work box, that's how, *mister*." He looked around the crowd to make sure they appreciated how he'd scored off the fuzz.

Joe ignored it. "Did he come in a truck?"

"I didden see no truck. I didden see him till he wuz up on the stoop and the ball bounced off him."

"He got hit 'cuz he didden look where he wuz goin'," the big boy growled as much at his friend as at the detective.

Joe searched the faces around him. "Anybody see a repair

truck on the street anytime this morning?" Again all he got was a regretful negative murmur.

"He could'a parked around the corner." Ted sneered for the benefit of his audience and to reinforce his story.

"That's a point," Joe conceded, bringing him along. "What did he look like?"

"How should I know? He had on a uniform is all."

"Was he tall or short; dark or light; thin, fat; young, old?" Joe started sharply, then remembered he must take it easy. "You've already demonstrated you have good powers of observation, Ted. I'll bet if you put your mind to it you'll be surprised yourself what a good description you can give."

"Yeah?" The boy frowned, aware all at once that though he was the center of attention, that though he was held in a kind of respect, it was wavering. He tried. "Well, he wuz old, like maybe thirty-five. And he wuz tall, taller than you but not so hefty like, and dark, but not dark as you, Sergeant. His hair . . . I didden notice his hair."

"Maybe you didn't notice it because it was covered?"

"Say . . . yeah, that's it! He wore a cap, one of those caps with—" he gestured—"a front."

"A visor?"

"Yeah!" Ted was really excited. "And his uniform was a light gray and real clean like he'd jist got it back from the laundry, you know stiff, with the creases still sharp?" His shrewd, sallow face twisted into a series of grimaces. "No . . . that uniform wuz a real light gray, and it wasn't even faded. It looked new. And you know what else, Sergeant?"

"No, Ted, what else?"

"His shoes wuzn't right!" The boy looked around him to make sure the crowd was impressed. "I went over ta pick up the ball at his feet and I noticed his shoes. They had pointy toes and a real good shine on 'em. They wuzn't work shoes."

"Nice going, Ted! Nice going. That's real sharp. Do you think you could recognize him if you saw him again?"

Ted went through the contortions that accompanied his thinking. Then slowly, reluctantly he shook his head. "If he wuz wearing that same uniform . . . No, sir, no, Sergeant, I'd reconize the uniform but not him. If he wuz to walk up to me right this minute, I woulden know him."

"Never mind, Ted. You've done very well. You've given us a lot to go on. I appreciate it." Joe smiled and held out his hand. "Thanks." Abashed, blushing, the boy hesitated. With an air of defiance at his buddy, he took it.

Joe's smile disappeared as soon as he got back inside. On the fourth floor the surly superintendent was still waiting.

"What kind of repairs were scheduled for Mrs. Broome's apartment this morning?"

"Repairs? What kind'a repairs you talkin' about, Sergeant?"

"I'm asking you."

"I don't know about no repairs. She didn't report no trouble."

"A repairman was seen entering the building around lunchtime. Who'd know about it?"

"Me. And there wouldn't be no repairman comin' here, Sergeant. I make the repairs. Unless it was utilities, like, say, gas or the telephone maybe, something. . . ."

He didn't finish because Capretto had already brushed by. *Oh, my God,* Joe thought, *he posed as the man from the telephone company! He could have said he'd come to check the new line, and she'd have let him right in.*

"Lieutenant?" Joe poured it all out into Felix's ear. Then he picked up the phone and dialed. It didn't take him long to find out what they already knew—no accredited repairman had been sent to that address that morning.

"So." Slowly Felix passed a hand over his chin. "Damn." He said it under his breath; nevertheless it startled Joe—the lieutenant wasn't given to even the mildest expletive. "Asa, I want anything you can give me on this, anything at all, and I want it fast."

For once the diminutive medical examiner didn't make a sarcastic parry. "Sure, Jim, I'll do the best I can."

Felix nodded to Cap. "Let's go." He glanced over to Norah. "You too, Mulcahaney."

\*\*\*

"Is he purposely drawing our attention to the phone calls? Does he want us to make the connection with the other two women? Is he issuing a challenge?" Felix asked as the three sat glumly in his office.

"Could be his mind is just stuck in that one rut," Cap commented.

The rain everyone had been praying for had begun. It beat on the window air conditioner like hail, but no one in the room seemed aware of it.

Joe took a deep breath. He didn't like what he was going to say. "Lieutenant, I don't think there *is* a connection between the deaths."

Felix's eyebrows shot up. "That's a reversal. Why not?"

"I just realized something. I should have caught it before, right away. She even made a point of it, Arabella Broome did, when she first reported the calls. I should have spotted it on my own, but I didn't. The guy couldn't have picked out her number at random from the phone book because she wasn't listed."

That snapped Norah out of her reverie. "She'd only been in the apartment three weeks. The phone was only just installed."

"That's it." Joe looked and felt miserable.

Norah was still reeling from the shock of finding Arabella dead. It didn't occur to her that her inclusion at the council a second time was vindication of her earlier judgment that the caller would move swiftly. To the contrary, in her own mind she deemed herself to have been not only as shortsighted as the others but wrong, too, for she had never considered actual physical danger to her new friend. She was grateful to be present because she wanted more than anything to help catch the killer, and being there meant she would have the official opportunity to try. Otherwise . . . well, no need to consider that now.

"The number belonged to somebody else before it was assigned to Mrs. Broome," she told them.

"He knew her name," Felix pointed out. "But check it anyway, Norah. Now. Use my phone."

Too concerned to feel selfconscious that both officers were watching and waiting, Norah dialed. She made her inquiries and got her answer. "The last subscriber to use that number was a Carl Zelinsky. He moved out of the city."

Felix leaned back. "So. He didn't pick it out of the phone book."

"She always maintained it was no stranger," Joe groaned. "I got hung up on the similarities between the three cases. Coincidences, I guess. So many damned coincidences."

"We did our best." Felix didn't seem any happier about it than the other two. He became brisk. "We go into her background and Buddy's and see what we can come up with. The way they were moving around it won't be easy, but it's still better than having to trace every anonymous, obscene, or crank call in the city. I'll admit I'm relieved on that score. So. All right, go ahead, Cap, get started. Norah, I'll arrange for you to stay on the assignment for as long as it takes."

She was too intent on the problem even to thank him. "Arabella Broome was killed because she put the police on the caller. If she hadn't tried to get the call traced, he might not have touched her. So there is a connection with the other two deaths."

"It doesn't necessarily follow." Felix remained gentle with her because he knew she was deeply affected.

"Why else would anyone want to kill Arabella Broome?" Norah pleaded. "She was the straightest person I ever met."

"Maybe the killer held her responsible for Buddy Broome's death?"

"How could he? Buddy was the addict."

"Weren't you the one who pointed out just yesterday that an irrational mind does not reason rationally?" Felix asked.

She flushed but wouldn't give up. "All right; then he blamed Arabella for her husband's death, and he was punishing her with the phone calls . . . just as he did with the other two." Norah floundered—she was on the verge of the truth but couldn't quite grasp it. "Arabella had been high at the time of Buddy's death, so she already had a sense of guilt about it. The other two women, Mrs. Emerson and Mrs. Neumann, felt guilty about their husbands' deaths. . . ."

"You're suggesting that a pervert happened to pick on three women each of whom had this guilt feeling over the recent death of her husband. That somehow he knew enough about each of them to prey on that guilt and drive two of them to take their own lives."

"And he was working on Arabella too, but she was too strong. She not only wouldn't succumb; she fought back. So he had to go over there and do the job himself." Norah quivered with excitement.

Jim Felix and Joe Capretto exchanged looks. Felix spoke calmly. "It fits, Norah, I don't say not, but it brings us back to the same stumbling block—he couldn't have got Arabella's telephone number without knowing her name. That blows the whole sequence. The other two numbers were in the book; hers wasn't. She claimed she didn't give it out to anybody because she didn't know anybody in New York. The only reason she had the phone installed at all was to . . ." His voice trailed off.

The answer hit them all at the same time.

"She did give it to him," Joe groaned. "Or as good as. She advertised it—in Buddy Broome's obituary. Oh, God! That's how he picked the other two *widows*—out of the obituary column."

"And that's how he'll pick out the next one," Norah said quietly.

# Chapter 8

"We already figured he was an old hand. Now it looks like somewhere along the line he had a near miss, called a woman who didn't live alone, who maybe even had a man—father, brother, lodger—in the house when he called. Maybe he's even been caught once." Cap assembled what facts they had as an identikit artist might collect assorted features to make up a portrait.

Outside, the rain was heavy. A strong wind rose, and with it a relieving cold front from Canada swept into the city. The night would be good for sleeping; it would bring surcease to the restless and an easing of tension in the ghetto streets. The entire department had been waiting for this help from nature, but not one of the three in Jim Felix's small office paid any attention to the rattling windowpanes.

Joe's dark eyes were half closed as he formed the mental image. "He reads the obits, and they tell him everything he needs to know: name, age, business of deceased; name of his widow and, most important, of other survivors. So he knows whether the intended victim is alone. He can gauge a hell of a lot more—her approximate age and circumstances. The address is right there, and he can look up the telephone number. In Arabella Broome's case she included the number in the notice, so Broome's people could contact her. He calls, and I suppose from the reaction he either goes ahead or drops it."

"It's not likely he'll change his MO," Felix decided. "The question is: Will the calls satisfy him now that he's got the feel of the actual kill?"

"We'll be watching the obits, too," Joe pointed out, "and

we'll be ready. Also the time gaps between victims is getting shorter. Ruth Emerson reported the calls to the telephone company about three weeks after her husband's death. We can assume she tolerated them for a couple of weeks before that. She jumped four days after her number was changed. That adds up to nearly a month. There was a hiatus of close to two weeks before Tom Neumann's obituary appeared, and Vicky Neumann killed herself within a week of that. It's only two weeks since, and he's already completed another full cycle. I don't think we'll have long to wait for the next one."

"Can we afford to wait?" Felix asked. "Can we afford to let him pick his next victim?"

Both Joe and Norah knew what he meant. They'd failed to protect Arabella Broome. Could they be sure of protecting the next one?

"I want to volunteer, Lieutenant."

"To do what, Norah?"

"To be the next widow."

"He's forewarned, Norah. He won't let you keep him on the line long enough for the call to be traced. We have to let him come to you."

"I know that. I want to do it, Lieutenant."

"All right. We'll fix you up with an identity, get you an apartment—you realize you won't be able to live at home for a while? Then in three or four days we'll plant the obituary notice."

"Suppose he doesn't bite?" Joe asked. "There'll be other obits; why should he pick Norah's?"

"We'll rig it so he can't resist. Both Ruth Emerson and Vicky Neumann were cheating on their husbands. Arabella and Buddy Broome lived together for a while before making it legal. Let's say Norah is a career girl in . . . television, that's a nice fecund field. Let's say she was about to get a divorce to further her career when suddenly her husband died . . . of an overdose of sleeping pills. That should give plenty of room for insinuation. It should also provide enough hint of scandal for the tabloids to give it . . . a page two splash anyway.

Maybe with a picture of the shocked and frightened widow?"

"Picture, Lieutenant? Suppose he was watching Mrs. Broome's place? He might have seen Norah going in and out. Wouldn't he recognize her? Aren't we taking a chance?"

"Even if he saw her, I doubt that he paid any attention to her. Certainly if he'd connected her with Mrs. Broome, he wouldn't have called while she was there. But let's play extra safe. We'll drape Norah in plenty of black veils; it'll make her look that much more vulnerable."

Joe looked doubtful. "Do widows wear veils nowadays?"

"Oh, a good Irish-Catholic widow might, eh, Norah?"

"I think a veil would be all right, Lieutenant."

"And we'd better have a funeral," Felix decided. "Very small and very private. It'll be interesting to see if anyone shows up."


Patrick Mulcahaney didn't like it, and he wasn't reluctant to say so. For once Henry Sorlein joined him in taking a stand against Norah's wishes. In fact, they had their first real quarrel over it.

Her cover had been set. She was Mrs. Norah Fogarty, a production assistant at NBC-TV: she would, after a few days of mourning, actually report for work and be given a desk and assignments. Her husband, Brian, had been an unsuccessful artist. They had already separated, though she had not yet applied for divorce, before his death. The newspapers would hint at his despondence over the separation and his wife's success, would imply suicide while intimating, though not accusing, Norah of responsibility. A furnished apartment under the name of Fogarty had been rented. It was in the East Sixties—Nineteenth Precinct—an area not so quiet as to inhibit a would-be attacker, yet not so lively as to offer him cover. She would move in tonight; tomorrow morning the story would break.

Norah was finishing her packing when the doorbell rang. She went to answer knowing it would be Henry but not expecting anything more from him than mild remonstrance and gentle exhortation to take care of herself.

As soon as she saw him, she knew it wasn't going to be that way.

"I don't want you to take this assignment."

It was close to an order. His voice, flat, impersonal, startled her. He had never spoken like that. He'd never looked like that either. He stood very straight so that he seemed taller than she, even though he wasn't. His pale fine skin, flawless as a woman's, was mottled with his displeasure. His small eyes usually so liquid that he seemed constantly on the verge of tears were absolutely dry and disapproving.

Norah recovered quickly. "It's not an assignment. I volunteered."

"Good. That'll make it easier for you to withdraw."

"Henry! I can't." Her jaw tightened. "I don't want to."

His attitude didn't soften. The surprise of his taking a stand and sticking with it this long put her off. She didn't know how to meet it. Then she sensed her father had come into the room; she could feel his presence behind her. She whirled. "You put him up to this!"

"If you mean I told him what you're going to do, you bet I did!"

"Don't I have a right to know?"

She was surprised at Henry's assertiveness, and she wavered. If she admitted his right, well, then, it was a commitment on her part, too, wasn't it? "It's a question of *my* right. I'm twenty-eight years old, I don't think I need to be told what to do."

"You're being set up as bait!" her father shouted.

"I'm not afraid."

"That's it. That's the trouble. I wish you were. We'd both feel better, Henry and me, if you had the brains to be afraid."

She would have liked to admit that she was in fact very much afraid, but that she also had complete confidence in the lieutenant's plans to protect her. But they shouldn't need to be told, neither her father nor Henry. They should try to understand that she was finally getting a chance to do something worthwhile, something useful. So instead of admitting what she felt, she pressed her lips tightly. "Thank you very much. Fortunately, the lieutenant doesn't think I'm a fool."

Sorlein's eyes were melting again. "Norah, your father didn't say that."

"It's what he meant. And you agree with him. Don't you?"

They glared at each other. Each wanted qualities from the other which the other didn't possess. Norah knew though that part of her sensitiveness was due to Arabella Broome's death, that she was at this moment emotionally unstable, that if she said any more now, she might regret it later.

But Henry too had second thoughts. "Forgive me, darling. I only want you to keep safe."

"I know."

He was kind and considerate, and Norah was glad she hadn't spoken.

Her father shuffled off to get her bags.

The next morning Norah put on her widow's black and went from the new apartment to the funeral parlor to sit in an empty room beside an empty casket. The story with her veiled photograph appeared in all the papers and got the minor prominence that the lieutenant had arranged for it. If anyone should show up to view the fictitious remains, he would have to identify himself, but no one was expected, and no one came. The period of the wake dragged, but Norah's excitement kept her from becoming bored.

The day of the interment was dark, one of those fetid days in which the clouds hung ominously, yet wouldn't give up their rain. Norah stood at the graveside with Joe Capretto as friend to the bereaved woman and a group of detectives as mourners while the empty coffin was lowered into the open trench. Then she turned away, and Joe solicitously walked her back to the waiting limousine. He put her inside, squeezing her hand. They would be in telephone contact, of course, but it would be the last time she'd see him or anyone else she knew until . . . until it was all over.

It wasn't till she got back into the city to the borrowed apartment and closed the door behind her that she was suddenly overwhelmed by the finalty of it.

The apartment was comfortable enough—living room, bedroom, kitchen, pleasantly furnished. There were books, radio, television. And she had lost no one; she was only pretending grief. Yet she felt a debilitating apathy. For the first time she had an inkling of what it must have been like for each of those three women to come back after a real funeral to an empty house and an empty life. She removed her veil and went into the kitchen to make a cup of coffee. She drank it slowly. It was only eleven in the morning.

Norah had never been truly alone. Though her mother died when she was only twelve, there had been her father and two brothers. Her brothers married and moved away, yet the ties remained strong, dependable. And, of course, she had her father's constant companionship. Now there was Henry, too, always available if she should decide she wanted him. This, she told herself, was just a taste of what it must be like to be so really alone that your existence didn't matter to anyone. Each of those women had faced it when she came back from the graveyard and closed her apartment door. It made those anonymous calls doubly cruel, doubly vicious, and, oh, so much more effective. It strengthened Norah's resolve to catch the perpetrator.

For now all she could do was wait. She tried to read—no good. She turned on the television—it didn't register. She could go out for a walk, but would a real widow do that the very first day? She decided not. She must have dozed because suddenly the television set was shining like a ghost in the shadowed room. She turned it off. She should eat, and that meant marketing, and it would be something to do.

Long after her meal was over and she had scraped half her

plate into the garbage, she decided to try the TV again—the Mets were on. She wondered if her father was watching. Was Henry with him? She realized now what her father had been trying to tell her these past years—she must make provision for the time when he would be gone. Quick tears started and were wiped impatiently and shamedly away. She went to bed at ten and fell asleep almost immediately.

She awoke in the dark feeling frightened and strange. It took a moment for her to remember where she was—the bed was on a different side of the wall; the streetlight came from the opposite side, too. She wasn't aware of what had aroused her till the phone rang a second time. It couldn't be *him*, could it? So soon! Maybe it was Joe—no, he'd be using the police extension. Her father then, or even Henry—no, and for the same reason; she must be really groggy. The radium dial of the clock beside her bed showed two ten.

The phone continued to ring.

She mustn't lose the call. Without sitting up or putting on the light she reached for the receiver.

"Hello?"

There was no answer. Had she waited too long? Had he already hung up? Of course not, the line was open. "Hello," she said again. "Who is it?"

Someone was definitely on the line and attentive, too—she could feel his concentration. *Is this the way it starts?* she wondered. Should I hang up? Normally, if this were happening to her, Norah Mulcahaney, that's exactly what she would do, hang up—hang up, forget it, and that would be the end of it. But now she was Norah Fogarty, widow of a man for whose suicide she might be considering herself responsible. Would Norah Fogarty hang up? And if she did, would he call again? She couldn't take the chance. She must go on talking in such a way as to encourage him, to give him an indication of vulnerability.

"Hello? Who is this?" Urgently and with a quiver in her voice which wasn't difficult to simulate she went on. "Please, whoever you are, why don't you answer? Why are you doing this?"

Still no reply, but Norah thought she could hear his breathing now, heavy, rapid.

*He feeds on his victim's terror,* she reminded herself, *so give him more terror.* "Please! I beg you, don't do this to me! I . . . I can't take it. I'm not well . . ." She pressed the button to activate the recorder. She must make him speak. "Please listen—I'm going to hang up now. I ask you not to call again. If you do, I won't answer. Do you understand? I won't answer!" She finished it on a rising note of hysteria.

"Ah . . ." A clearing of the throat. "Ah . . . Look, miss, I'm sorry. There's been a mistake. Please don't be upset. I've got the wrong number. I'm sorry."

The surge of elation when he began to talk died instantly. Wrong number? He wouldn't go through that surely? What would be the point? But he did sound genuinely embarrassed, apologetic, and his voice was certainly pleasant.

"I'm very sorry," he repeated.

"Why didn't you say you had the wrong number? What were you waiting for?" She was angry and growing angrier partly in reaction and partly in disappointment. She was becoming too belligerent for the part. "You frightened me half to death. You know that, don't you?"

"I didn't realize it at the time, I mean that I had the wrong number. I thought . . . well, you sounded so much like Ellen, I thought you were Ellen. . . ."

"Why didn't you speak then?"

"I guess I owe you an explanation."

"You certainly do."

"Ellen's my girlfriend, well, *was* would be more accurate. We had a date tonight, but she claimed she didn't feel well. I know she went out with another man. All night I've been agonizing about whether I should call her up and tell her I know. It would mean the end between us, but obviously it's over anyway, so I dialed and you answered. Then suddenly I felt foolish, embarrassed, giving the thing too much importance, giving her too much satisfaction. . . . All this time, of course, I thought you were she, and by the time I realized my mistake . . . well, I was even more embarrassed."

"Oh." Norah didn't know what to make of it. It was logical, and he sounded sincere. The situation was somewhat similar to that between Henry and herself. Certainly it was a strange way to start a series of nuisance calls, much less the kind of call she was expecting. "What's your name?" she asked abruptly.

"Robert Ellis."

He'd answered promptly; it didn't mean it was his real name. She'd better keep it going for a while longer, anyway. "I'm Norah Fogarty."

"Well, Miss Fogarty. . . ."

"Mrs. Fogarty. My husband died. I buried him today. That's why I reacted so hysterically." Norah went ahead confidently now because she had an idea to test him. "You see, he died from an overdose of sleeping pills. The newspapers, well, they hinted . . . they have to make the story interesting, I suppose. I've been getting crank calls and so . . . well, I just jumped to the conclusion that yours was another one of them."

"Oh, look, Mrs. Fogarty, that's just awful. I can't tell you how sorry I am that I upset you like that. Have you notified the police?"

"What could they do?"

"I'm sure they could do something. Trace the call. . . ."

"I'm told that takes considerable time."

"Well, have you thought of changing your number?"

He sounded legitimate! And she didn't know whether to be glad or sorry. "I guess that's the best solution. The thing is, he'll probably turn around and bother somebody else, but I can't help that, I guess."

"You have to look out for yourself."

"Yes, well, good-bye, Mr. Ellis."

"Mrs. Fogarty? Ah . . . would you mind if I called you tomorrow? Please don't misunderstand . . . I . . I'd just like to make sure you're all right."

"It's not necessary."

"I know that, but I'd like to."

Norah hesitated an appropriate interval. "If you want to. Good night."

A tracing device had been attached to the telephone merely as routine since it wasn't anticipated that after his scare with Arabella Broome the killer would stay on the phone long enough to make use of it. In her report Norah glossed over the fact that she hadn't turned it on. She assured herself he really hadn't been on the line all that long.

Just the same she had a hard time getting back to sleep.

His name really was Robert Ellis. By the time he called back, just after ten thirty the next morning—so she could make up the lost sleep, he explained—Norah had a make on him. He was thirty-five, single, a junior account executive at Barlow, Borden, and Dunbar. He was considered a "bright young man." Everyone liked Robert Ellis: He "kept his nose clean"; he was "always ready to do a favor." In a business in which drinking is almost unavoidable he managed to be almost a teetotaler without offending. Nobody knew much about him outside working hours. He lived alone on Eighty-fifth Street just off Lexington Avenue. Except for his approach, he could be the man they were after.

Four days went by, during which, aside from her contact with Joe by telephone and the nightly telephone checks by her father and Henry, Robert Ellis' calls were the only break in the monotony. She came to look forward to them. The friendship grew to the point where Norah began to wonder what would happen when the case was finished and she resumed her own identity. She didn't question the likelihood of still being in contact with Robert Ellis, only the manner of her explanation. Subconsciously she had absolved him. She also began to worry about how much longer the lieutenant would allow the stakeout to continue. Worst of all, she worried about what the killer was doing in the meantime. Since he hadn't picked her out of the obituaries, had he chosen someone else? Was some genuine young widow at that very moment being taunted and debased? Joe reassured her; there had been no likely prospects in the obituaries during those long four days. She supposed the lieutenant would let her continue till a genuine prospect turned up.

Meanwhile, Robert invited her out to dinner. She refused, pleading the impropriety of accepting an invitation so soon after the funeral.

"Go," Joe instructed during a conference on the special line, "but meet him at the restaurant; don't let him into the apartment. I think you've got yourself an admirer, but let's play it safe. It's barely possible that by going out with Ellis you might stimulate the real psycho into action. If he's watching your place, it could be just the nudge he needs. I'll have a tail on you from the time you leave the building, so don't worry."

It was eight o'clock on a fine, fresh August night with a tang in the air presaging fall. It felt good to be out, to be walking in the city's twilight glow, to be going to meet this man whom she felt she knew so well, though until the real culprit was actually caught, he must remain a suspect. He was waiting for her under the canopy of the restaurant. They recognized each other from half a block away.

"Norah."

He took her hand. Each looked and was pleased at what he saw and sensed the other's approval and pleasure.

Robert Ellis was a little under medium height, but Norah didn't consider that a fault. He was one of the handsomest men she had ever met—blond, blue-eyed, broad-shouldered. Maybe he was a little thin; he looked tired, maybe he'd been ill—but otherwise. . . . Why should any girl stand him up? Why should he involve himself with a blind date? Well, this wasn't strictly a blind date. The handsome Ellis' obvious delight in her swept Norah's faint misgivings away.

The restaurant was not what she had expected either. It was small, pleasant, but brightly lit and bustling.

He caught her surprise and commented on it. "No one could object to your coming to a place like this." She nodded. "And the food's not bad either." He smiled broadly.

It was, in fact, very good, though she noticed he didn't eat much of it. She did, though, enjoying herself so much she almost forgot to look around for the detective on duty. Not recognizing anyone made her feel a little less selfconscious, but she still knew that someone was there, that she herself was on duty, that she should be trying to draw Robert Ellis out. Her constant attempts to do it over the telephone had been hard enough; having to do it now face to face after all the trouble he'd gone to to please her made her feel guilty. And the more he tried to put her at her ease, the worse she felt.

"What's the matter?"

"Nothing."

"You haven't said a word in the last five minutes."

"Oh? I'm sorry. I didn't realize. I . . . I was thinking."

"What?"

She decided it was easier and would be better later if she stuck as closely as possible to her true feelings about him. "Well, you're a good-looking man. I'm sure you don't have any trouble getting dates. So why did you bother calling me up all this time? I could have been . . . a dog."

"I knew you weren't."

"Still. . . ."

"What about you? Why did you bother with me?"

"You know my situation—those stories in the papers. Most of my friends were Brian's friends too. If I went out with any of them, it would give the stories substance." She was forced back into the lies. Then, almost wistfully she tagged on a bit of truth. "I was lonely."

He seized on that. "Me, too. I've never been married, but I came close once. It didn't work out. The disappointment ... well, I've been careful about getting involved again."

"How about Ellen?"

"Ellen? Oh, Ellen was just a girl I took out a few times. I wasn't serious about her. I just didn't like being made a fool of. I'm not likely to get serious again easily." He looked across the table at Norah. "Talking to you like that on the phone without ever having seen you, I got the feeling that I knew you better than any of the girls I've taken out. I got the feeling you were different. And I was right."

Norah bowed her head; she couldn't look at him.

Dinner over, they walked the ten blocks back to her apartment companionably side by side but not even touching hands and with only occasional spurts of conversation. In the lobby of her building he faced her standing so close she thought surely he meant to kiss her, but he only stared as he had done in the restaurant.

"I'll call you in the morning, all right?"

She nodded, and he turned his back on her and walked out.

She had hardly got upstairs, in fact, was just turning on the bedroom lights when her doorbell rang. Who could that be? Nobody from the department was supposed to come near the place. Had Robert changed his mind and come back? Who else? After he'd been so exemplary in the lobby? She went to the front door but didn't open it.

"Yes? Who is it?"

"Norah, it's me."

"Henry!" She let him in quickly. "What are you doing here? What's happened? Dad! Is he all right?"

"Yes, yes, of course, your father's fine. I was worried about you."

"Me? What for?"

"You didn't answer your phone."

"Is that all?"

"Isn't that enough? You're alone up here, messing in

something you don't understand, inviting assault, and you don't answer your telephone at ten o'clock at night."

"I didn't realize it was after ten."

"Considerably." Henry Sorlein glared. "Who was that man who came into the lobby with you?"

"You saw us? Where were you? I didn't see you."

"You're not the only one who can play detective."

"I'm not playing."

"All right, I'm sorry. I didn't mean that." But he resumed the interrogation. "You still haven't answered my question. Who was that man?"

She shrugged. "A suspect."

"You didn't treat him like a suspect."

"I wasn't supposed to."

"I didn't know you were going to come into actual contact with any suspects. You told me all you were going to do was talk to him on the telephone. I won't have you exposing yourself to God knows what kind of unbalanced, perverted...."

"I'm not. I wasn't. We were under observation the whole time. I won't have you skulking in doorways and spying on me."

"I didn't see anyone keeping surveillance."

"You're not supposed to see him. And you're not supposed to be up here."

"And you weren't suppose to go out with anybody either!"

They were shouting at each other. Both realized it at the same time, and both stopped. Again Henry was the one who offered a truce.

"What should I have done when I kept calling and there was no answer?"

Norah sighed. "You could have called Sergeant Capretto."

"I see."

"Well, he would have told you there was nothing to worry about."

"He knew all about it, did he?"

"Of course. I told you. . . ." She didn't finish—it just seemed useless.

Sorlein met her silence with a stolid silence of his own. But pointedly he made an inspection of the room. "Nice place. Very nice, when you consider all you're supposed to need is a telephone. How much longer is this going to go on?"

Norah sighed. "I don't know."

"Are you going to make dates with every nut who sees your name in the newspaper?"

"Oh, Henry. . . ."

"Are you?"

"If I have to."

"What do you expect me to do meantime?"

So once again the challenge was down. Well, why not be honest and admit she didn't really love him, at least not with the irresistible intensity that Norah associated with love that led to marriage? She felt twinges of that kind of attraction toward Joe Capretto, but she suppressed them considering herself not his type, not sufficiently feminine and vacuous to suit him. It was with Robert Ellis that she felt most nearly right. Every good sense warned her she was taking a chance letting herself get involved till the real killer was caught; every tender instinct proclaimed the impossibility of Ellis' guilt. So wouldn't it be only fair to release Henry? Nor could she tell herself that this was not the moment for it. It was exactly the right moment.

"That's up to you." Again Norah had temporized; again she'd settled for holding on to Henry just in case. . . . Was she now, after the days as Norah Fogarty, so afraid of loneliness that she was prepared to settle for Henry just for security and companionship?

"I'll think about it," he replied and went to the door, walking out without a backward look.

She watched him—stunned. Good, reliable Henry, even he had a point beyond which he would not accept humiliation. So she'd lose him anyway and have the added shame of being the one jilted. She sighed and headed back to the bedroom.

Slowly she began to undress. Her brooding was interrupted by the telephone. That would be Robert! Her spirits lifted instantly. He would just about have got home by now and would be calling to say good-night. All the self-doubts were dissolved in her eagerness to speak to him.

"Hello!"

"You couldn't wait, could you?

The voice was not Robert's. It was not any voice she had ever heard. It was an ugly voice, hoarse and hollow and evil. A shiver of fear and excitement went through her.

"You couldn't stay loyal even a week. Not even one week. And two men on the same night. You make me sick, you filthy bitch."

# Chapter 9

Norah sucked in air and then held it. Her body went rigid. She listened helplessly to the voice that was angry and at the same time sad. As though he were disappointed in her. As though he didn't want to say the things he said. She didn't know how long he talked, but she heard him out because she couldn't do otherwise. When he hung up she stayed as she was, the receiver clamped to her ear till her bursting lungs demanded release. Then, gasping, she lowered her hand to the cradle. She let the receiver clatter into it. That triggered the realization that it was over and brought the cold sweat all over her body.

Then she remembered the tape recorder.

Robert Ellis crossed the street and waited for the lights in Norah's apartment to go on. He hadn't offered to go up with her because she might have thought he was going to make a pass. After the unconventional way they'd met he didn't want to give her even a moment's uncertainty about him. But he had to be sure she got in all right; nowadays the most respectable buildings were vulnerable, and a doorman in the lobby was no guarantee that some mugger or worse might not be lurking in the upstairs halls.

While he waited, he examined the three hours they'd just spent together. Robert Ellis hadn't enjoyed anything so much in a long time. He hadn't met anyone like Norah in a long time either. She was . . . decent. Her marriage had been a mistake, a young girl's mistake of giving her love to the wrong man, a man who hadn't valued it. Selfish and self-centered, wrapped up in his so-called art, that's what Brian

Fogarty had been. Ellis had nothing but contempt for the pseudo artists. Look at the way Fogarty had let his wife go to work to support him! Oh, sure, Ellis had read those news stories about the suicide with their snide allegations about Norah, but he knew enough about reporters to grasp when a story was slanted for reader interest—scandal was what people bought at the newsstands with their dimes. Ellis hadn't mentioned to Norah that he'd seen the stories. What purpose would it have served? Now that he'd met her he was glad he'd kept his mouth shut because he knew now for sure that she was innocent of any responsibility in Fogarty's death. She had done her best to make the marriage work. Look how loyal she still was. She refused to say one unkind word about her husband. And look how reluctant she'd been about accepting a simple dinner invitation in a public restaurant. A girl like that could really help a man. Could make him pull himself together.

Only one thing bothered Robert Ellis about Norah—her being in the TV field. She wasn't the type. He knew a lot about TV, advertising and entertainment going hand in hand as they did. And he'd met plenty of eager young actresses, production assistants, "gal Fridays"—all out to make it, all willing to barter, pushing every minute. Those girls didn't do a thing without the primary motive of *what's in it for me?* Norah wasn't like that. She was straight.

Seeing the lights come on, Robert Ellis smiled and turned away, but not before he caught sight of the man entering Norah's building. The man looked familiar. He'd seen him before that same evening. He was sure of it.

"So?" Lieutenant Felix raised his perpetually arched brows a little higher.

"She wasn't tailed, Lieutenant," Capretto assured him. "If anybody was watching the building, he didn't follow her here."

"Okay." Felix looked at the girl. She was tired and drab in her widow's black. But the difference went deeper; she simply wasn't the self-confident, self-assertive young woman who had argued righteously in that office ten days earlier. He supposed it was the actual contact that had shocked and chastened her. He wondered how long the salutary effect would last. "Well, Norah?"

"I typed up a report, Lieutenant." She opened her large policewoman's handbag and took out the folded sheets and laid them on his desk.

Felix went through them quickly. "So." He looked at her sternly. "I hope you told your boyfriend that he jeopardized the whole operation by barging in like that."

"Yes, sir."

"I'll admit that your date with Ellis plus your boyfriend's visit triggered the caller into action. But Mr. Sorlein is not to visit you again—under any circumstances."

"I told him, Lieutenant."

"The important thing here is that *he* had to be watching. Unless it was Ellis who called."

"Oh, no!" Norah gasped.

Felix raised his eyebrows at her, then looked his question at Capretto.

"Schmidt stayed right with Ellis, Lieutenant, and Ellis went straight home. He could have called from there, of course...."

"It would make the timing one more coincidence," Felix remarked sourly.

"It wasn't his voice," Norah insisted.

"He'd disguise it, naturally. Unfortunately, since you didn't get a tape, we can't run a voice profile comparison. I'm not blaming you, Norah; I realize it happened fast."

Norah's cheeks burned.

"I am inclined to agree, though, that it wasn't Ellis. It seems more logical that whoever it was had been keeping watch, and as soon as he saw Sorlein leave, he went to a booth nearby and called. Were your shades up, Norah?"

"I'm not sure. I'm sorry, Lieutenant."

"There's a drugstore on the corner, Lieutenant, just across

the street," Joe explained. "If he's going to keep watch on her, so can we. As soon as Norah gets the next call, she can give a signal—pull down one of the shades, say. We move into the drugstore and spot whoever's using the phone."

"Because he's called from there once doesn't mean he's going to do it again," the lieutenant pointed out.

"If he continues to keep watch on her, sir, then I'd say the probability of his using the nearest available telephone is high. It looks to me as though he's building on the hints we planted in the newspapers about Brian Fogarty so that he'll have material with which to confront Norah and he will go on watching."

Felix frowned. "I suppose we have to give it a try. How many booths are there in the drugstore?"

"Three, but as soon as he hangs up, Norah can raise the shade," Joe hurried to forestall further objections. "It's hardly likely that the actions of more than one out of the three possible users will tally with both signals. So we move in. Meanwhile, Norah has got her tape, we get another and compare. Simple."

"Simple is right. What do you suggest we then charge him with? Committing a nuisance?"

Joe flushed. "No, sir. So we don't move in. We tail him and find out who he is and check his alibi for the morning of Arabella Broome's death."

"That's more like it." Felix nodded.

The ring of the telephone is a mechanical device. The tone of a particular instrument never varies, nor does the interval between rings. How was it then, Norah asked herself, that at ten minutes after eleven that night when her phone rang she knew instinctively that *he* was calling?

She had moved the telephone close to the window so that she could easily reach the shade if it should be necessary. Once inside the booth *he* would no longer be able to see her, but Joe in his car or at the front of the drugstore would. Only now as she reached to pull the shade she couldn't see

Joe anywhere. She panicked. Where was he? What had happened? Had they changed their minds about the scheme? Surely they would have let her know?

The phone kept ringing.

Then the man at the rack of paperbacks in the store window raised his head. She recognized him from the slant of his shoulders and the shock of dark hair. That was Detective David Link. Norah was reassured, though still puzzled. She lowered the shade and picked up the receiver.

Clifford Harmon lifted the receiver, put in his dime, then hesitated. Why should he suddenly feel guilty? Why should he suddenly feel sorry for her, pity her even? She deserved no pity; she'd brought it all on herself. All right, now she'd have to take the consequences. He didn't like what he was doing, never had, but it was necessary. There was no other way. Clifford Harmon was so upset he misdialed and had to hang up. Then he couldn't get his dime back. So that meant fishing for change. In the process of sorting it the whole handful clattered to the floor. Squirming in the confined space of the booth to retrieve it, Harmon could feel his heart pounding. He came up flushed, breathing hard. None of this was doing him any good. The doctor had warned him against excess strain or emotion. He was in no condition to make the call, but he would make it. All he needed was a few moments to calm down. Let that guy pacing outside use one of the other booths.

Jerry Pepper knew she was waiting for the call. He would have known even if she hadn't snatched it up on the first ring. He would have known it from her short, shallow breathing that made his own breathing quicken. As he talked, he felt all the tensions slip away. It was good to be able to say all the things he'd been thinking all day, storing up for her. He visualized her face as she listened. . . . The thought that he couldn't even call her directly from home but had to come out to use a public booth was enough to bring a surge of resentment that nearly ruined the moment's satisfaction. But he must be patient. He must not spoil everything by being careless, not now. He must take every precaution for just a little while longer. Soon though, he consoled himself, very soon....

Reid Loudon spoke as though by rote. It was in fact a formula. The girl made the expected responses, but he hardly listened. At the beginning he had got a kick out of their whining, pleading. Then the calls had been enough almost in themselves, had given him a sense of power. Now he took that for granted and was impatient. He even admitted to himself that the calls were not strictly necessary, yet he continued to make them because he'd always done it that way—and why change a winning game? Reid Loudon smiled to himself in the telephone booth, but the smile was quickly gone. Calling it a game was only an expression. This was no game. Far from it.

Joe was delayed getting to the drugstore. As the result of the check of vantage points from which Norah's apartment could be seen, Lieutenant Felix had a new idea he'd wanted Joe to investigate. Joe pulled up at the curb just in time to see Norah's shade go up. He hadn't expected the call to come so early in the evening. He bounded across the curb and entered the drugstore.

David Link had moved from the paperback racks to the counter and was sipping a Coke. He and Capretto had worked together plenty of times; they had an instinctive rapport. So all he had to do was glance casually to the rear. Following the look, Joe saw the doors of two booths opening almost simultaneously. David must mean they'd both gone in at the same time too—lucky he'd arrived in time to help.

The first man out was close to fifty, the responsible citizen type. Not portly, but close to it and aware of it, for he held himself erect and stiff as though sucking in his stomach muscles. His hair was thin and a suspiciously even brown. His eyes were narrow. His sharp nose lined up exactly with the cleft in his chin to give him a cunning look. Whatever the call had been about, he was still absorbed in it and headed straight for the exit looking neither to the right nor to the left, probably not even seeing what was directly in front of him.

The other who came out of the adjoining booth was young—nineteen or twenty—nice-looking but with an adolescent's skin. He walked stoop-shouldered with the selfconsciousness of the tallest boy in the class. Just a kid.

Joe glanced at David. Link put a hand up to scratch his cheek and the thumb and first two fingers were extended.

Three? Oh, no! But from David's worried look Joe knew it was true. How in hell were they going to divide three into two? At that moment the last of the booths opened, and a male fashion plate stepped out—turtleneck shirt, dark wraparound glasses, deep tan contrasting with frankly graying hair, a diaphragm as lean and hard as the boy's. Three—one of them already out on the street.

Joe nodded and David slipped from the stool to follow the boy. Of the two men Joe would have to let one go. If he were lucky, of course, one might get into a cab or car; then he could get the license number to check later and follow the last of the three on foot. If both elected to walk. . . .

Joe moved to the drug counter where he could get a good view of the sidewalk. "Packet of aspirin," he told the clerk. It wasn't an idle purchase. He needed it.

# Chapter 10

Link had no trouble following the kid—he walked fast, never looking back. He didn't go far either—around the corner to Park, then across and straight over to Third without detours or any attempt at evasion. At Third he crossed again. There was a massive apartment building at the corner. He went past it at an even brisker rate so that David following him at a gap of half a block because of the nearly deserted situation wasn't prepared for his sudden ducking into the doorway. He closed in soon enough to see him hunch over the keyhole, turn the knob, and slip inside. The detective broke into a run. By the time he got there the door was not only closed again but locked.

The door was steel, painted black with white lettering —SERVICE ENTRANCE. Naturally at this hour it would be locked. But the kid had used a key.

Link stepped back and looked up at the rows of anonymous windows. None of them lit up obligingly to indicate where the suspect had gone. He could be an employee, but would his entry have been so furtive then? If he was a tenant, how did he come to have a key to the service door? And why?

David thought it over. It would be simple to go around to the front and find the doorman. A description would undoubtedly get a name and an apartment number. He wasn't supposed to alert the subject, but Link was always inclined to take the direct course. Also, he had hunches—good ones, the lieutenant himself admitted it. Every instinct told David Link that if he got the kid's name now and went up, he'd catch him off guard. The next few minutes could be worth hours of plodding work later. He needn't say that he'd followed the boy from the drugstore. He'd have to find a pretext though. . . .

The doorman was old with the curiosity of one whose own life was dull and who resented his position. "The kids have it too easy nowadays" was his explanation and solution for the entire youth problem. He put a name to David Link's description of the boy quickly and positively: Jerry Pepper. Had to be. Too tall to be anybody else. He lived in 10F. Only child. *College boy.* It was a label—pejorative and envious at the same time.

Standing in front of 10F and ringing the doorbell, Link still hadn't worked out what he was going to say. The peephole was opened, and a man's voice asked, "Who's there?"

"Police officer, Mr. Pepper." He was trusting that the situation inside would indicate the line he should take, but he was starting to sweat all the same.

The door was opened on a chain. *Even in this fortress they're afraid,* Link thought.

"You have identification?"

He showed it and was admitted.

He passed through a square foyer that was as large as his own living room and into a salon, no other word for it, formal, expensive, not only in the original cost but in the maintenance. Every surface was polished; every ornament glittered. The Oriental carpet glowed with color.

"Mr. Pepper?"

He was a fat little man with dark jowls, the kind that never shaves clean. He was in shirt sleeves and slippers, and he'd been watching the late news on television. The picture was still on, but he'd turned down the sound.

"Sorry to disturb you, sir—" Link began.

A woman's voice called out. "Jerome? I thought I heard the bell. . . ."

She stopped at the threshold of the inner hallway. She sounded nasal and haughty, and she looked the way she sounded. She wore a kind of blue jersey robe trimmed at the

sleeves and hem with dark fur that could be, probably was
. . . sable? Head held high, she advanced into the room bosom first.

"Mrs. Pepper? Sorry to disturb you, ma'am," David began ingratiatingly. "Actually, it's your son I want."

"At this hour of the night?"

She was the kind, Link guessed, who went on the offensive immediately, instinctively, on general principles. He gave her one of his best and most deprecating smiles, but he knew the response to that gambit—counterattack. "He is home, isn't he?"

"Certainly." Her thick lips puckered into a prissy line. She acknowledged his move and made her next play. "He never goes out on a school night."

Link let that pass. "If I might speak to him?"

"He's asleep. His light went out nearly an hour ago."

Link made a point of consulting his watch.

The flesh whitened above the puckered lips. "He's been studying hard. He gets up in the morning before six. With all the disruptions they've had up there at Columbia there's a lot of work to make up. Jerome is an honor student." She took personal credit for it.

Link could have hugged her; she'd given him the clue he needed! Now he could get on with it. "That's what I wanted to talk to him about." Link gazed blandly at both parents. "If you would ask him to step in here for a few minutes. . . ."

But Mrs. Pepper would not relinquish command. "Are you suggesting that our Jerome is in any way connected with that shameful business? Because I tell you categorically that he is not. You cannot prove otherwise. Whoever gave you his name did it only in pique because he refused to join in, because he's against SDS. He was so disgusted with it that he actually wanted to transfer out of Columbia. But I—that is, his father and I . . . well, why should he be forced out of the school of his choice? Why should he have to go away to a strange city and live in rented rooms when he has his own comforts here at home?"

115

She was writing the script for him. Link suppressed his delight. "On the morning of September twenty-third there was a demonstration by students from various city universities in front of the UN. Perhaps Jerome mentioned it? Or perhaps you read about it?"

"Neither. The press and television make too much of these student pranks. It gives them an importance they wouldn't otherwise possess. They should be ignored."

Well, he wasn't going to argue it out with her. "This was an orderly demonstration, Mrs. Pepper, perfectly legal. It was intended to show that students can behave responsibly and thoughtfully. That opposition need not be violent to make a point. Your son took part in it."

"I don't believe it!" Myra Pepper's bosom heaved indignantly. "Jerome wouldn't. Under any circumstances. That's slander."

Jerome, Sr., waved her to silence. "If it was all so orderly and legal, why are you here?"

"Unfortunately an outside group broke up the demonstration. There was injury and serious damage to property. Now if your son is really against this kind of violence, he'll want to give us the names of any members of the other group that he recognized."

"He wasn't there...." Myra Pepper reiterated with the first quaver in her assurance.

But having let his wife do the talking, Pepper, Sr., took the action. He walked out of the room. Moments later he returned with his son.

Junior was in pajamas, his feet half out of his slippers, still fumbling with the sash of his robe and blinking sleepily. It was a good act; it might have fooled David if he himself hadn't been the one who'd followed Junior through the dark streets from the drugstore on Madison Avenue.

"This is Detective Link of the New York Police, Jerome," his father announced. "He wants to ask you some questions."

Obviously the boy was taken by surprise, but instantly on guard. He couldn't hide his wariness, and his parents saw it as plainly as Link did. Instinctively they moved closer together.

Now David hesitated. Should he give him his rights? This was the gray area in which an officer was allowed a certain leeway. Certainly young Pepper was a suspect, but only one of three. What Link was after was information, and in that instance he wasn't required to advise him of his rights. Later on, if it appeared that Jerry was indeed the guilty one, then of course he'd have to. It was a dilemma often faced by an officer. He knew, of course, what the lieutenant would do, play it safe. But playing safe wasn't David Link's way.

"Where were you on the morning of September twenty-third?" he asked abruptly, hoping to take advantage of the youth's momentary confusion.

"September twenty-third?" Junior repeated dully. "I don't know. I'd have to look at my calendar. Why? What happened on the twenty-third?"

*Murder happened,* Link thought. It was why he had chosen the particular date. *On September twenty-third at or about noon a girl was strangled in her bed on West Twenty-first Street. Maybe that date means something to you, and maybe it doesn't.* "A group of students from universities in the city staged a demonstration in front of the UN," he said.

Junior's confusion seemed complete, but he was still careful.

"It was a peaceful demonstration until an opposition group broke it up. We want your help in identifying the leaders of the militant faction." Link waited.

The boy looked from his parents to the detective in a puzzled way. He frowned, then sighed. "I wasn't there."

"Where were you?"

"I suppose in class. What day was the twenty-third?"

"A Tuesday."

"That would be Contracts. Contracts IA."

Link gave him one more chance. "How is it your name was given to us as being in the demonstration."

"You've got me." He shrugged, but he was still thinking hard.

"Look, if you're afraid of informing, if you're afraid of reprisals...."

"No, it's not that. It's just...." Jerome Junior took a deep breath and made his decision. "I wasn't there."

Mrs. Pepper's matronly flags were unfurled again. "I told you he had nothing to do with it."

"Yes, ma'am."

"Whoever put Jerome's name on that list of yours just wants to get him into trouble."

Link looked at the boy. "Why should anyone want to get you into trouble?"

Mrs. Pepper had resumed full charge. "There doesn't have to be a reason, just general hostility to anyone who's normal and decent, that's all."

But David Link didn't take his eyes off the boy, whose answer again was a helpless shrug. Link threw up his hands. "That's it then. I guess that's as far as we can go here." He smiled engagingly. "Sorry to have disturbed you, folks. Thank you and good night." He walked out.

David Link was well satisfied with the results of the initial interview. Contrary to his implication in bidding the Peppers good night, this was not the end but the beginning of his investigation into young Pepper's nightly activities. He had offered the kid an alibi, a strong one. The kid had sniffed it, pushed it around, had seemed on the verge of biting, then had drawn back. Was it because to substantiate his presence at the demonstration he'd have to name names and he didn't want to? Or couldn't? If he'd been on the other side of town September 23 committing murder, he could have thrown names of a few known student agitators at Link—he wouldn't have been getting them into any more trouble than they were already in—if after committing murder he still had qualms about anything so relatively minor. Or maybe he was smart enough to spot the trap, to remember that on that Tuesday, September 23, there had been no student demonstration at the UN or anywhere else.

And what about the parents? Something was bothering

them all right, and it wasn't that the boy might have participated in a peaceful march.

Tomorrow David would go up to Morningside Heights and check the class attendance records. For now . . . well, he figured there was no use hanging around: Jerry Pepper had enough of a scare to lie low at least for the rest of this night.


Joe Capretto paid for his aspirins and got to the door of the drugstore just as the cab pulled away. It was the responsible citizen who had hailed it, and Joe had got a good look at the license number. If he didn't go straight home, at least he might get off at a point where he could be traced. Okay, now he could concentrate on the other one, the male model. He was already about two blocks up Madison and walking energetically. No problem catching up, only to do it without alerting him. There weren't many people out; on the other hand, the street was relatively dark, so one thing balanced the other.

Joe had shortened the distance between them and settled into the pattern of a casual stroller when his subject ducked into a bar.

*Hell!* Joe thought. He could call in and have somebody else take over but there wasn't a street booth in sight. Nothing for it but to stay on the job himself. The only available cover was a nearby doorway. It would have to do.

It wasn't long before his subject sauntered out again. He walked straight to the curb as though he too now wanted a cab, or was it a ruse to take a look around? Hopefully the former. Just then the lights changed, a bus that had been caught in traffic two blocks back came roaring to a stop right where the male model was standing. He got on. Joe cursed. He waited as long as he dared. If he got on too, he was bound to be noticed, now and later when they both got off again. It was that or lose him irretrievably. Joe charged out of his shelter.

He made it. While he fumbled for a token, the hiss of air indicated the front and back doors were closing. Cap put the fare in the box and started toward the rear in time to see his man step across the gutter onto the sidewalk. The bus started.

*Oh, God!* Joe thought. *I've been had.*

By the time Clifford Harmon got home he was feeling better. He put his key in the lock, and as he opened the door, the blare of the television assaulted him. Damn! Why did she always have to run it so loud? It would have been too much to hope that Grace would be out tonight. He just didn't have that kind of luck. He put his briefcase down beside the console in the hall.

"Clifford? Is that you?" she called mixing incredulity, pleasure, and suspicion in equal parts.

*Who else?* he felt like answering. *who bloody else?* Instead, he walked over to where she sat and, leaning down, placed a dry kiss on her forehead.

"You're early." The same blend as before with an added pinch of accusation.

"We had sandwiches delivered instead of breaking for dinner so we could work straight through."

"How virtuous you all must feel!" she sneered. Her skin had the familiar sausage-tight look, but her eyes were as yet only partially glazed. She wasn't drunk, but she was well on the way.

"I don't know what you mean by that."

"Giving up an expense account meal to get home early is the supreme sacrifice. I didn't know there were so many devoted husbands on the board." Usually she kept the liquor hidden and never actually let him see her drinking. But she hadn't been expecting him, and the glass was beside her, so instead of trying to hide it, she picked it up and brazenly gulped. "You must have been outvoted."

"I come home late, and you complain. I come home early, and you're sarcastic. What do you want, Grace?"

Her unfocused eyes filled with tears of self-pity. "Honesty. That's all. For once in your life I want you to tell me the truth."

He looked at her bloated face and flaccid body—and remembered. He shook his head. "No, that's the one thing you don't want." He turned and started out.

"Cliff! Cliff? Where are you going?" She pulled herself up. Using the back of the sofa to steady herself, she groped after him. "Cliff, don't go. Please. Don't leave me."

"I'm only going down for a paper."

She swayed slightly, but she accepted it. "You won't be long?"

"As long as it takes me to get to the newsstand and back." But his sympathy had given out. "I'm not planning to run."


Joe showed the driver his ID and was let off in the middle of the next block. It was too late, of course. The man had disappeared—into one of the side streets, or back in that bar, or in any building to wait it out. The area was principally residential—no skyscrapers, but nothing under fifteen stories either. He could check the doormen, but how about the buildings without doormen? If his man had caught a cab, he might be ten blocks away by now and in any direction. Joe heaved one of his energizing sighs and got no lift out of it whatsoever. All that was left was to go through the motions. He walked to the nearest entry.

An hour later he gave up. It was five minutes before one. The cabdriver who had picked up suspect number one at the drugstore would have gone off duty probably. If Joe could contact him and get the address from him, it might temper the report he'd have to turn in to the lieutenant in the morning.

He started back to where he'd left his car. It would have been great to have been able to walk up to each of those men using the phone booths and ask each what number he'd been calling and check it out. But as the lieutenant had said, it would have been a short cut to a dead end. Instinctively, Joe looked up at the windows of Norah's apartment. Dark. She'd be asleep. He unlocked his car and got in.

Up to now two things worried Joe because of the night's

fiasco. The first, that the man he'd tailed and lost was both caller and killer. The way Joe had been lucking out on this case, what else? After all, your innocent upstanding citizen isn't likely to be looking to be followed, and if he should by some ineptness on the detective's part catch on . . . well, he has no experience in shaking a tail. But Suspect Number Three, the male model type, had shown plenty of experience. The second worry was that by botching the tail, Joe had driven him to cover.

Now a third possibility occurred to him.

Suppose it had the opposite effect? As it had had in Arabella Broome's case?

This time the victim would be Norah.

# Chapter 11

Joe had a nervous, scratchy feeling between his shoulders, a feeling that someone was behind him. There couldn't be. He'd approached from the other block, through the building backing on Norah's, checked the fire escapes and the halls too before knocking on her door.

"Joe?" she whispered.

"Let me in."

The chain rattled; the door opened on darkness. He sidled through.

"Do you think he's watching?"

He hadn't told her what it was about. He'd called on the special line to alert her that he was coming and also to warn her to keep the lights off. Once again he had to admire her perception.

"No use taking chances." He shrugged again. Joseph Antony wasn't one to brood for long over what couldn't be helped. "No!" He put his hand over hers as she reached to put the chain back on. "You've got your bedroom window locked, haven't you?"

"Yes."

"Well, we don't want to make it impossible for him, do we?"

"I guess not," she quavered. Now she had it all.

He still held her hand. "This one's real easy, Norah, believe me. No sweat. The front door's the only way in. *If* he comes, I'll be sitting right here waiting."

"You don't think he will come?"

"I don't think he's the B and E type; neither does the lieutenant. I'm here as a precaution. In the morning, well, that's something else. Maybe we'll see another repairman or salesman . . . who knows? Or maybe we won't."

"You wouldn't be here if you didn't expect him."

Joe tried to reassure her. "He was in contact with his victims for several days of intensive abuse. The calls increased in frequency and nastiness before anything happened. So far you've only heard from him twice, and each time he was relatively mild, right?"

"I suppose so."

"I don't think he's worked up enough yet. The pressure hasn't built to the point where the calls themselves can no longer provide adequate relief."

"I thought we decided he killed Arabella Broome because she tried to have him caught?"

Now that his eyes had grown accustomed to the dark Joe could not only see Norah's face, but could read the changes on it. Again, she had understood without being told. Norah standing against the light from the street saw that she was right, but she sensed there was more to it. "I watched you and David leave the drugstore and go separate ways, so there are two suspects. I guess you've covered yours, and if Link is on his, won't we get a warning?"

He hated to deprive her of this slim comfort. "There were three men using those booths when you gave the signal, and all three finished at the same time—more or less."

"And there were only two of you."

"That's it." No use going into how he'd botched his assignment, not now. Why add to her fears? Later on . . . she had a right to know. He made himself as brisk and cheerful as possible. "Anyhow, no use in both of us losing a night's sleep. You go back to bed."

"No."

"You do what I tell you."

"I don't want to. I wouldn't be able to sleep."

"You're an obstinate woman, Norah Mulcahaney. But I'm a determined man. Let's not fight."

"I'm not fighting. . . ."

He took her by the shoulders and pulled her to him and kissed her, making a good job of it. She was startled, then angry, resisted, and finally went limp, deciding to wait it out.

"Well now, if you want to stay here in the dark with me all night, we might as well be friendly—and comfortable." He pulled her over to the sofa with him and sat her down. He put his arms around her.

Norah wrenched herself free and jumped up. "You're on duty here, Joe. Have you forgotten?"

"It would help me to remember if you put some clothes on."

"Oh!" Instinctively Norah clutched at the folds of her robe. Then she smiled in the dark. Joe was teasing her—wasn't he? "You want me to put my uniform on?"

"I want you to get the hell into the other room!" he snarled.

"All right, *Sergeant!*" She flounced away, spoiling the exit by crashing into a small end table, recovering to pull the door shut behind her forcibly but also remembering not to slam it.

It wasn't long before Joe heard the creak of the bedsprings. Alone in the dark, he grinned. Now she had something besides murder to think about.

Norah's alarm went off at six forty-five as usual. She was instantly alert. With daylight time still in effect and fall upon them the mornings were slipping irretrievably into darkness. Norah hated getting up in the dark. This morning she didn't even think about it. All her attention was on the closed door and the man on the other side of it. Last night's indignation, embarrassment, and—admit it—excitement all came back. *Don't think about it, go about your business,* she warned herself. But she couldn't; the very fact that Joe was there called for an adjustment in the simplest action. Ordinarily, for instance, she would have gone straight out to the kitchen to put on coffee. But that meant passing through the living room. So she charged into the bathroom instead and turned on the shower. She was in and out in minutes. She dressed as quickly as she ever had in her life, not into uniform, of course, but in her widow's black. It wasn't particularly becoming. She brushed her hair impatiently and wound it into its usual knot, which refused to lie straight, and made do with lipstick for makeup. She didn't look like much. Defiantly she threw open the bedroom door.

He was gone. She gaped, deflated. The room was very neat, neater than she'd left it the night before. That made her angrier—was he trying to show her up in everything? Then she wrinkled her nose—coffee? Did she smell coffee?

"Hi! I got tired of waiting, so I started breakfast." Joe leaned against the kitchen doorframe, cheerful and bright as though it were all perfectly normal and natural. "What took you so long?"

"What took me so long?" she sputtered.

"I'm kind of anxious to get in there myself, you know." He indicated the general direction of the bathroom.

"Oh. Oh, I'm sorry. I . . . I didn't think."

"Okay. Here. . . ." He tossed the dishcloth at her. "I'm really not much in the kitchen. Make it three eggs for me, once over lightly." He put his hand up to his chin. "I don't suppose you have a razor?"

"No, Sergeant, I don't get calls for one."

"Girls use razors."

"I know you get around. You don't have to prove it."

He wouldn't have let her have the last word except that the phone rang. They both jumped, then relaxed—it was the police line. "I'll take it," Joe said and marched into the bedroom.

Mostly he listened. His only comment was an occasional grunt, but Norah, who was watching, noted that his handsome dark face turned an ugly yellow and his soft jaw tightened and she knew something unexpected and bad had happened.

"Get your coat," he told her as soon as he'd hung up.

"What about breakfast?"

"Forget it. We're to report in. Right now."

"Me too?"
"You too."

"We're in trouble."

It was out of the ordinary for the lieutenant to call them all together, so the men in the squad room were soberly attentive. The bald announcement stopped the most minute scrapings and rustlings.

Jim Felix's eyes engaged each man in turn. He seemed as usual—serious, cool, but his men recognized the signs of agitation: the abrupt spurts of pacing; the drumming of fingers as he paused and leaned against a desk; the green eyes narrowing as he made a point; the determined set of his long, square jaw.

"You know that we've been very cautious about mentioning the obscene telephone calls as a possible connection between the Emerson and Neumann deaths and the Broome homicide. We've made a point of keeping that aspect out of the newspapers." He paused, then added, "For reasons which I'm sure are obvious to you all." He paused again. "Somehow it's leaked."

If possible the silence deepened.

"Pete Laperriere of the *Post* picked it up. He's already connected the Broome homicide with the murder last night of Carmen Piñero."

Norah gasped; Joe glared at her; Link sighed. The other detectives remained silent and grim. Felix chose to address Norah.

"That's right, Mulcahaney; another young widow was murdered last night."

Because she'd been the one being watched and protected! Norah thought.

Because he'd opted for a few hours' sleep instead of keeping tabs on Junior! Link thought.

Because he'd been gulled by the oldest trick in the book! Joe thought.

"As I said, Laperriere has latched onto the similarities

between this homicide and Arabella Broome's. To begin with, both were strangled, both were young, both recently widowed and living alone without friends or relatives, and"— Felix paused significantly—"both had been receiving anonymous telephone calls."

"Carmen Piñero did not report the calls, but she did confide in a girlfriend. Because of what the caller said, she thought she knew who it was." There was an eager stirring through the room. "I'll come back to that later." Everyone subsided.

"Now I pointed out to Mr. Laperriere, or Peep, as most of you know him, that the similarities could be coincidence, that there was no connection or association between the victims. I asked him not to print his speculations. He agreed. Most of you know how reluctant Peep is to sit on anything for long and how nervous he gets on the pot."

There was a brief ripple of amusement, a break in the tension.

Felix acknowledged it, then cut it off. "I don't know how long he'll stay quiet. Also, just because Peep has promised to hold off writing the story doesn't mean he's going to hold off asking questions. To the contrary. He's not called Peep for nothing. Once he connects these two homicides with the two other deaths . . . God knows nothing will keep him quiet."

Was that an admission that he himself now connected all four deaths? Norah got no pleasure from it, no satisfaction in the vindication.

"When that happens, Laperriere will quote the bit about 'responsibility to the public,' and he'll be right. On the other hand, I don't want the women of this city thrown into a panic. I don't want every phone crank having a field day, and I don't want our switchboard swamped with hysterical women reporting every wrong number and demanding police protection. But the women do have the right to know there's a psychopath loose and that each and every one of them is in danger. They have the right to know, so they can take precautions."

Brennan cleared his throat. "Up to now hasn't it been only widows?" A logical man, guided by facts, he didn't panic easily.

"Right. But once the story breaks, we'll have a rash of imitative crimes, and I doubt very much they'll be limited to widows or spinsters, to young, old, pretty, ugly. . . . There's only one way to stop it. You all know the answer—get the killer."

Felix resumed his pacing in the tight circle between desks, then picked up a sheet of paper where he had put it earlier on the desk nearest the door to his office. "Let's get the specifics:

"The latest victim is a Mrs. Carmen Piñero, age twenty-six, married one year. Husband, Juan Piñero, was killed in a construction accident just eight days ago. The obituary appeared three days after the Brian Fogarty one. So it looks like he knew from the beginning the Fogarty obituary was a plant."

Once more Felix paused, looking around the room. "Doc Osterman estimated Carmen Piñero died between four and six this morning. Mrs. Piñero was in her nightgown, wearing a robe but no slippers. The bed had been slept in, but she was killed four feet from her front door. The killer was facing her."

Link, ever mindful of his early Safe and Loft days, spoke up. "She wouldn't let a stranger in at four a.m."

"You wouldn't think so," Felix agreed. "Particularly since she'd been getting the abusive calls. But there were no signs of forcible entry front or rear. The building entrance is locked at midnight, but there's a handy fire escape that can be reached from a back alley." He frowned, then sighed. "Now did he wake her as he came through her bedroom window and was she running toward the front door to get away from him? He could have stepped in front of her, barring her way out; that would account for her facing him when he strangled her. In that case, would she have stopped to put on her robe? It seems more likely that she got up in answer to a quiet knock and let him in herself."

"He'd have to have access to the building—that means a key, and that makes him a tenant," Roy Brennan concluded.

"Nobody in the building saw or heard anything; they claim they were all asleep—which at that hour is reasonable enough. Still, they're pretty clannish up there in Spanish Harlem; it could be that they're covering up. I get the impression the marriage was . . . ah, let's say, tempestuous. Juan Piñero was a jealous man, and his wife had plenty of boyfriends before they got married. Some say afterward too."

"Maybe she was expecting a visitor and the wrong man turned up." Link's eyes gleamed.

"Could be." Felix looked at the burly Czech who had considerably simplified his name. "Poll, find out."

"Yes, sir."

"Cap, the man who took the Yellow Cab is Clifford Harmon, 101 Central Park South. He's yours."

Joe nodded. The lieutenant didn't need to say it—it was hardly likely the man they wanted had taken a cab directly to his home address whether he'd known the drugstore was being watched or not. He'd shown he was much too experienced for that. No, the killer was the man Joe had lost.

"Before you go over to see Harmon, get an artist to make up an identikit picture of the other one. We'll put out a flyer."

It was remarkable how the lieutenant could keep pace with his men's mental processes. "Yes, sir." No more would be said, but for Joe it was a heavy reprimand.

"David." Felix went on with the assignments. "You stick with Junior."

Link stepped forward jauntily. "Nothing to it, Lieutenant. That is as far as the morning of the twenty-third goes. All I have to do is go up to Columbia and take a look at the attendance records, if there are attendance records. But last night . . . well, evidently he's been slipping in and out the rear service door at will. He has a key."

"Did I say it was supposed to be easy?"

"No, sir." Link stepped back into line with the other men and stared down at his well-shined shoes.

"Emmerling and Groat, follow up on Mrs. Piñero's boyfriends. Schmidt and Charlton, backtrack on the two suicides, go over everything from the beginning." He clapped his hands. "So. Let's get moving. Oh . . ." It was almost an afterthought. "Mulcahaney, you contact Ellis and get that number he was allegedly calling when he got you instead." Felix's frown now included Joe. "I don't know how we all overlooked that. All right. After you get the number, Mulcahaney, pack your stuff and go home."

"Home?"

"Somehow, somewhere along the line, one of us gave the show away."

Felix's look hovered between Capretto and the policewoman. "The caller not only knew you were a decoy but used you to divert us. Now you're no good to either side."

Norah went from scarlet to white. It wasn't being removed from the case that upset her, though of course that was a deep disappointment, but the manner of it. The lieutenant had stated a fact: Norah was no longer of any use. But his harshness implied negligence. She looked instinctively to Joe. She found sympathy, but what could he do? Not one of the other men in the room made a sound. The very absence of reaction revealed the shock that each man felt. The lieutenant had had occasions, plenty, to chew an officer out, even to remove an officer from a case for cause, but he'd always done it with consideration for the officer's feelings—meaning he'd done it privately. To humiliate a young woman—it was unprecedented.

"Take the rest of the day off," Felix added. "Tomorrow

report back for your regular duties." As though he knew that it hadn't softened the blow, he turned his back abruptly on Norah. "Cap," he snapped, "in my office. The rest of you, I want reports on my desk by four."

Definitely, the lieutenant was not himself.

# Chapter 12

Clifford Harmon came to his office the following morning in a condition of cautious optimism. He attended to the early routine, his confidence reinforced by its accustomed dullness. Then his secretary announced that a detective wanted to see him, and the morning exploded around him. Like a flooded engine, his mind stalled, his muscles locked, and his throat constricted so that he couldn't speak. The pain in his chest made him double up. Nothing could be proved, he assured himself. Nothing. He blinked a couple of times till the spiraling whorls of color in front of his eyes faded, till the office righted itself, till he could look around and draw the usual measure of reassurance from its conservatively luxurious appointments. It was an outward indication of the position he had worked so hard and sacrificed so much to attain and from which he would not be lightly dislodged. *Easy, take it easy,* he cautioned himself. He poured a glass of water from the dull pewter decanter and took one of his pills. Better, much better. Now. There were plenty of other things it could be. Maybe a traffic ticket? He never took chances parking illegally, but Grace. . . . Maybe it was about Grace! Maybe she'd got into trouble in a bar? Wouldn't that be a laugh? What a handle it would give him. He started to chuckle, then became aware that the intercom was still open. He hadn't spoken aloud, had he? That was a bad habit, one more thing he'd have to learn to control.

"All right, Miss Millet, send the detective in."

His voice had been steady and authoritative; Clifford Harmon regained some confidence from that. He was able to greet Joe Capretto expansively.

But Joe was no novice—he could smell the animal fear. It determined the tone he would take. Flipping his ID perfunctorily, he started right in, formal but tough, that would be the line.

"You were present in an area and at a time in which a crime was committed recently. You may have seen something that could be of help to us."

"Oh." Harmon swallowed his relief. He was wanted as a witness. Then he became wary. It could be a trick. "What kind of crime?"

"I'm not at liberty to give you details."

"Then how can I help?"

"By answering a few questions."

Harmon shrugged and waved the sergeant to a chair. "I'll do what I can, naturally. Naturally, I want to cooperate."

"I was sure you'd feel that way, Mr. Harmon. Now . . . last night at approximately eleven ten you made a call from a drugstore on Sixty-sixth and Madison."

*Oh, God! Oh, God,* Harmon thought, *it couldn't be any worse.* "Damn it to hell, what business is it of yours?"

Joe raised an eyebrow as though shocked at the violence of the reaction. "That depends on who you were calling."

"I'm not going to answer that."

"You don't have to, Mr. Harmon." It was time to inform him of his rights. "Do you understand these rights as I've explained them to you?" But the routine had panicked Harmon—as it often did the most innocent witness, paralyzing, so that it was nearly impossible to extract any useful information.

"It's an invasion of privacy," Harmon recovered enough to sputter.

"As you say, sir."

"Why do you want to know?"

"I'm sorry, Mr. Harmon, I can't tell you that."

"It would seem then, Sergeant, that the interview is over." Harmon got up.

Joe rose too, courteously. "I'm afraid not. I have to ask

you to come with me. You'll be able to contact your lawyer, of course, as I explained."

Harmon was sweating; he knew he couldn't hide his anxiety. "I want to cooperate, Sergeant; I've said so. If you could tell me what connection a phone call that I made from a drugstore...."

Joe decided to give him a little rope. "Where were you the morning of September twenty-third?"

"September twenty-third?" Harmon repeated the date, trying to appear vague but giving away that the date did indeed have significance for him. "Let's see, that would be after Labor Day, of course . . . I'd have to consult my appointment book. My secretary...." He reached for the intercom switch, then stopped. "Oh yes, I remember, yes. I was in Chicago on business." Eagerly now he fumbled through the pages of the desk calendar. "Yes, yes, here it is. Yes." He spoke slowly, pausing between each scrap of information. "So I'm afraid I can't help you after all, Sergeant."

Joe remained unperturbed. "We have reason to believe you were in New York that morning."

"Your information, wherever you got it, is not accurate."

"Can you prove you were in Chicago?"

"You can check the hotel register."

Joe dismissed that with a wave of the hand. "It's a short flight from Chicago to New York. You could have made the round trip within the morning. The hotel register wouldn't show that."

"I don't have to prove I was there. You have to prove I wasn't." Harmon folded his arms and sat back.

"We're prepared to do that."

Harmon would have liked to smile, but he couldn't. "Where am I supposed to have been?"

"On West Twenty-first Street."

"Doing what?"

"Visiting a woman named Arabella Broome?"

"Who's Arabella Broome?"

"The woman who was murdered on the morning of September twenty-third."

Harmon's small eyes bulged; the constriction around his chest returned. He brought a sweating palm across his mouth, and it left a wet trickle on his chin. "I don't know anything about any murder. I've never been on West Twenty-first Street in my life that I can recall. I never heard of any Arabella Broome." He recovered enough to shift from defense to attack. "Why pick on me? How did you get my name?"

Joe sighed. "You said you wanted to cooperate."

"I'm trying to, damn it! I can't say I was there when I wasn't. I can't tell you anything unless I know what you want."

"You could tell me who you called from the drugstore last night."

"All right, all right, all right! Before you jump to God knows what outlandish conclusions. I called my secretary."

"Why didn't you call her from home?"

"Because I hadn't got home yet," Harmon replied with heavy patience. "We had a board meeting here in the office. The switchboard closes after five thirty. I have no direct outside line."

"I see."

"No, you don't. There were some instructions I had to give her as a result of the meeting. She wasn't present—we keep the meetings strictly confidential. But there was some work I wanted her to do first thing in the morning as a result of the meeting."

"I see."

"Ask her!"

"All right. If you'll call her in."

"Now?"

"Please."

Joe hadn't looked at her a second time when he'd entered —he did now. She was about twenty-two to twenty-five, nice-looking, with all the right assets, but nothing spectacular. Still, for a man like Harmon. . . . He held up his hand to forestall Harmon's coaching her.

"Miss Millet, is it?"

"Iva Millet."

"Miss Millet, did you receive any phone calls at home late last night?"

"Yes, sir," she answered promptly. "Mr. Harmon called about eleven. There were some letters that he'd dictated and that were supposed to go out first thing in the morning. He wanted to make some revisions. He told me to hold them."

"Ah. Now on September twenty-third, Mr. Harmon was in Chicago. Is that right?"

"Yes."

"Did you have any communication from him?"

"I was with Mr. Harmon."

Joe looked at the businessman. "You didn't mention you took your secretary with you." Joe evinced gentle surprise.

"I didn't mention I took my tape recorder, or which charts or presentations I carried, either."

The girl flushed.

"Miss Millet accompanies me on all my trips. She's indispensable."

"All right, Miss Millet, so you went to Chicago with Mr. Harmon and you returned?"

"On Wednesday, the twenty-fourth."

"And where were you the morning of the twenty-third?"

"Me?" The hesitation was so normal and at the same time so slight that Joe almost overlooked it. "I spent the morning in my room at the Ambassador East transcribing some notes and getting out the letters."

"And where was Mr. Harmon?"

This time you could have put a picture frame around her uncertainty. She looked to her boss for help, but whatever message he was silently telegraphing she failed to receive. "I really don't know. He mentioned some business appointments and a lunch. He told me after I'd finished the work, I could take the rest of the day off."

"And when did you see Mr. Harmon again? The next morning on the flight home?"

"On, no, that night. He took me to dinner. In the Pump Room." She smiled, completely relaxed. "It was wonderful."

Smart girl, Joe thought, really smart. There was a lot more to Iva Millet than could be discerned even with several looks. She was admitting what couldn't be concealed and leaving the door ajar for the rest . . . though it would probably cost Clifford Harmon plenty if he should want it opened for Joe to take a look.

"Did you see Mr. Harmon at all the morning of the twenty-third?"

"Yes, sir, we had breakfast together downstairs in the coffee shop, and he laid out the work."

Capretto turned to the executive. "You still have no alibi for the time of the murder."

"Murder!" Iva Millet cried out.

Harmon glared first at her, then at the detective. "Are you through with Miss Millet?"

"For now."

"What does that mean?"

"It means you could save a lot of trouble by telling what you were doing the morning of the twenty-third."

Harmon jerked his head at the girl. "All right, Miss Millet." He waited till she was gone and the door firmly closed. "Look, Lieutenant. . . ."

"Sergeant."

"Sergeant. Look. We both know what I was doing that morning and with whom. Now I'm a married man, and I hope you'll keep that in mind and give me a break."

"What about Miss Millet? She made it quite clear that you were not in her room at any time."

"Well, what can you expect? Miss Millet has her own reputation to protect. But I suppose if it's absolutely necessary. . . ."

*Sure*, Joe thought, *and if you pay her enough*. "I don't think so, Mr. Harmon. Her unsupported word has no value.

We'd require confirmation, witnesses who saw you together —a waiter, chambermaid, like that."

Harmon went white. "There was nobody."

"Too bad you were so discreet."

Harmon gulped. "It looks like a standoff."

"Maybe not. Let's go back to last night. After you called Miss Millet, where did you go?"

"I went home. You can ask my wife."

They knew that, of course, it was how they'd got on to Harmon. "And stayed home the rest of the night?"

"Yes. Well, I did go down for a newspaper. But that took only minutes."

"And your wife will confirm it?"

Harmon wiped his chin, and it remained beaded with sweat. "She'd fallen asleep by the time I got back."

"She didn't waken? Not even for a moment?"

"No."

"Won't she even say she did?"

Harmon glared, then began to tremble. His whole body was out of control. It took what seemed like minutes and every bit of willpower for him to stop. "She'd been drinking." The admission revealed years of bitterness. "A brass band wouldn't have waked her."

For that at least Joe pitied him, but he had to continue the pressure. "Maybe the doorman saw you come back. You do have a doorman?"

"He wasn't around."

"There's always Miss Millet."

"We've covered that, I think. Anyhow, what's so important about last night? What happened?"

"Murder. A second time."

Clifford Harmon looked around at his luxurious office, the image of his labor and of his success, and saw it disintegrating.

"I think I will call my lawyer."

The registrar's office referred David Link to the particular professor who kept an attendance sign-in sheet, and Jerry Pepper's name was on it. Since he already had an alibi, why had he been so tempted by the one the detective had offered?

Then David smiled; some days it takes awhile to get with it. Today was one of them—warm, sunny, typically Indian summer—a day that swaddled the mind in its euphoria. You had to shake loose to concentrate. He left the Administration Building and set out across the campus humming cheerfully, blissfully unaware that he was as usual off key.

The lecture hall was actually a small amphitheater. There was one entrance and four marked exits in the semicircular rear wall. You signed in, and nobody noticed or cared whether you stayed. So, end of problem.

New problem: What did Mr. and Mrs. Pepper think young Pepper had been up to the morning of the twenty-third? Not participating in any demonstration—Link would have put money on that. But they were afraid he hadn't been attending classes either. Why?

According to the morning's schedule, J. Pepper, Jr., would be coming out of his first class at ten fifteen. Link headed back to his parked car. Then he changed his mind. There were plenty of empty benches around. Why not sit and wait and enjoy the day? He picked a bench near a recently planted sycamore, a young tree that did not block the sun, and slid down to the end of his spine till he could lean his head against the backrest and stretch out his legs. In this ironing board position he closed his eyes and came close to dozing off. The sudden clamor of changing classes roused him. The mall was crowded. Where was Pepper?

Ah, there, about fifty yards ahead and moving purposefully, dodging around and between slower, more leisurely groups. In a hurry, the kid was definitely in a hurry and headed off campus.

He never looked back. He was either innocent or dumb. He crossed Broadway. It occurred to David Link that Junior might have a car parked nearby, and he regretted his own indulgence in enjoying the sun instead of sitting in his own car, ready on the instant. But his already legendary luck held—Pepper kept on walking with that same determined stride. He zigzagged a few blocks and then abruptly and unexpectedly ducked into a small luncheonette. As there were plenty of eating places much nearer the school, it appeared that young Pepper had come to meet someone.

Link looked the place over—one entrance, counter in the front, booths in the back. Pepper went directly to the back and chose a booth. How about an exit through the kitchen? Since the kid knew him, Link couldn't very well go in. He pulled back. The block was almost exclusively residential. There was a bus stop at the corner; it offered the only excuse for loitering. From there he'd be able to see Pepper's booth and he didn't dare go around the corner to check the kitchen exit either. . . . He began a slow stroll to the corner—he had no choice.

Fortunately it was the lull between the breakfast and lunch rush, and there was little traffic in and out of the restaurant. From time to time Link wandered back to peer through the glass front for a glimpse of Pepper. After half an hour, still alone, the kid began to show signs of dejection. Link decided to make his move.

He walked in boldly and was actually sliding into the banquette opposite before the boy was aware of his presence.

Jerry Pepper's reaction was instant and aggressive. "What are you doing here? What do you want?"

"I was just going to ask you that."

Contemptuously, Pepper gave the empty plate a shove and pointed at the half full coffee cup. "You've got eyes."

"Long way to come for a snack."

"So? I don't go for those campus hangouts. Too much togetherness. Forced jollity. Who needs it?"

"Kind of a loner, are you?"

"Something wrong with that?"

"Depends on what you do when you're alone."

Pepper frowned. "What's that supposed to mean?"

"Nobody lives in a vacuum. Everybody wants to be the center of his own universe. If he can't be in the real world, then he invents a world of his own." *The job's turning me into a philosopher,* Link thought.

"Are you saying I'm some kind of a nut just because I come over here for some peace and quiet?"

"What kind of world have you created for yourself, Jerry?"

"I don't know what you're getting at; I'm no good at riddles." He half rose to slide out of the booth.

"Where are you going?"

"I've got a class."

"No, you haven't; you've already cut it." Link pulled out the typewritten schedule he'd obtained. "It was your last class of the day."

"Okay. So I just don't want your company. Is there a law that says I have to sit here?"

"No. You can come downtown with me if you'd rather."

Pepper remained as he was, half up, half down, leaning on the table so hard that his palms left sweaty imprints on the plastic top. "Why are you bugging me? I told you last night I don't know anything about any demonstration. I can't give you any names. So get off my back."

"I know you weren't there."

"You do?"

"There wasn't any demonstration."

That brought Pepper down again. "I don't get it."

"I want to know where you really were the morning of the twenty-third."

The boy sighed. "Oh, hell."

"I've checked the class records; I know you signed in. How do I know you didn't walk right out again?"

"Why would I do a thing like that? It's crazy. You can't prove I did."

He seemed like a nice young guy—well mannered; serious, maybe too serious; reserved; antagonistic, but weren't they all antagonistic these days? There were no traces of the sickness, of the taint of which Link suspected the youth, but something was certainly wrong. "No, I can't prove it. But it may come to the point where you'll have to prove you didn't."

Pepper craned his long scrawny adolescent neck. "What's so big about the twenty-third?"

David decided to lay it on the line. "A girl named Arabella Broome was murdered."

"Who's Arabella Broome? Was she in one of my classes? Am I supposed to have known her?"

Link could have sworn it wasn't put on. "We have reason to believe you're involved."

"Me?" The boy just stared. It took a while for the glaze to melt into fear. "Are you putting me on?" Then he reverted to wariness. "Did my parents put you up to this?"

David was shocked. "Your parents?"

"No, no, forget it. Listen, forget I said it. I mean, I don't know what made me think such a thing. Listen, I panicked. Who wouldn't?" He paused, trying to recover. "All right, so there's been a murder, but what's it got to do with me? I mean, this girl, Arabella Broome, I never even heard of her. Who says I knew her?"

"Last night at eleven ten you were in the drugstore at Madison and Sixty-sixth. You made a phone call. Don't bother to deny it—you were seen by me and another detective."

"There's no law against making a phone call."

"It depends on who you called."

Pepper only looked sullen.

"Why didn't you call from home?"

No answer to that either.

"Why have you been going down to the drugstore nearly every night for the past month to make your calls? The clerk remembers you. Why couldn't you call from home?"

"That's my business."

"Not anymore it isn't. Before she was killed, Arabella Broome was getting anonymous telephone calls." Link waited. "Obscene calls."

"Oh, God . . ."

"I followed you last night when you left the drugstore. Why did you sneak into your own building through the back? How come you have a key to the service entrance? Why don't you want your parents to know you're going out at night?"

The kid was deeply shaken, but he held. "You said the girl was killed on the twenty-third. That's over two weeks ago. I couldn't very well be calling a dead girl."

"Did you go out a second time last night, Jerry? After I left your apartment, did you sneak out through that service entrance one more time?"

"No."

"Can you prove that?"

The boy only shook his head.

"That's too bad." Pepper waited. "Another girl was killed last night. She'd been getting nasty phone calls, too. Her name was Carmen Piñero."

Jerry Pepper spoke quietly without hope of being believed. "I don't know her either. I never heard of her."

# Chapter 13

"I didn't kill anybody. I went to class the morning of the twenty-third, and I stayed the full period. The telephone calls are my own private business."

Lieutenant Felix met Jerry Pepper's hard stare with a level one of his own. "Not one of your classmates remembers seeing you when the period ended."

"That doesn't mean I wasn't there."

"Suppose I tell you we have a witness who saw you somewhere else? At the scene of the crime."

The boy swallowed. His nice, attractive face was very frightened, his voice cracked with the strain, yet he managed to forget his awkwardness about his height and sit very tall and sure. "All right. Bring him in."

Jim Felix was impressed. He leaned back, knees crossed, and rocked. Innocent or guilty, that had taken courage. But the boy was hiding something, no mistake. It was the quality of his resistance that troubled Jim Felix—he showed neither shame nor indignation at an accusation that combined perversion with homicide. It was more as though he were fighting a delaying action or . . . My God! the realization hit the lieutenant with the impact of the obvious: He's protecting someone else!

Felix looked over to see if it had occurred to David Link, Link who was usually intensely intuitive.

The lieutenant's arched brows lifted as high as they could; he sighed in assumed resignation. The boy had already heard his rights read and remained unmoved; would he remain unmoved to impending arrest? "Book him," he told Link; then to the boy he added, "I suppose you'll want to call your parents."

"My parents? Why do they have to know?"

"I don't think you understand, Jerry. You're being arrested on suspicion of murder."

The boy's face twitched.

"Once you're booked everybody will know. It will be in the newspapers. Whatever you did or didn't do on the dates in question will be open for public speculation. In fact, your whole life will be public. Your friends will talk about you and wonder about you, your fellow students, your teachers; the background people—doormen, merchants, the bus drivers —they'll all be experts on Jerome Pepper, Jr. You think your parents can be kept out?" Felix paused to let it sink in.

"Now if it's something really private," he went on, "something you want to keep from your parents but that has nothing to do with the crimes we're investigating, well, it doesn't have to go any farther than this office."

He was tempted; Felix could see it. Without taking his eyes off the boy, the lieutenant sensed that Link too had got it at last.

"You have my promise," Felix added quietly.

Pepper's young face was contorted with indecision. He looked miserable. "On September twenty-third at eleven thirty in the morning I was down at City Hall. Getting married."

Jim Felix was excellently trained in not revealing his reactions, but this time it was very hard. He glanced sideways at Link, who was having his own troubles looking blank. Felix decided to relax and broke into a broad grin. "I don't know what I expected, but it wasn't that. And your parents don't approve, is that it?"

Jerry Pepper nodded, more distraught than he had been at the prospect of arrest. "They want me to finish school."

"Aren't you due to graduate in June? That's not so long, is it?"

"There's more to it. For one thing, Laura isn't social enough for them. Besides, her parents are against it, too. They don't want her to get married at all; they want her to have a career as a concert pianist. The way things are now . . .

well, maybe you think we're squares, but she . . . well, she's old-fashioned and she wanted to get married." Then he added part apology and part challenge: "And I want her to be happy!" He paused. "She's only seventeen, so her people could get it annulled. But we figured that if we went ahead and she got pregnant . . . well, neither side could do much about that, could they?"

"And?" Felix asked.

The boy flushed. "I don't know. She went to the doctor yesterday, and when I called her last night, like I do every night, she said she wouldn't know the result of the test till morning." He turned to David Link. "If it was good news, she was going to meet me in the luncheonette. She didn't come . . . so that means no."

"I'm sorry," Felix said.

"That's okay. We'll keep trying." Jerome Pepper, Jr., blushed furiously.


"You have no actual evidence, Lieutenant, none at all." Alexander Maynard stated it with unruffled assurance.

The lawyer sat beside his client, Clifford Harmon, in front of Jim Felix's desk while Joe Capretto stood to one side in back. Maynard spoke patiently as though he were trying to assist both parties. Not a prepossessing figure—squat, pasty-skinned, with dark jowls that hung loose like a hound dog's dewlaps—he was meticulous in the freshness of his linen and the press of his suits and the luster of his fingernails. He affected sober serge and then paired it with shatteringly colored shirts and flowing psychedelic cravats. Something for everyone. He was respected for shrewdness and practicality. Felix did not underrate him.

"You've picked up my client because he made a telephone call in a specific place at a specific time. A flimsy pretext at best, besides which Mr. Harmon has explained the call, and his secretary has confirmed the explanation."

"It's not enough," Felix countered.

"Are you suggesting that both Mr. Harmon and Miss Millet

are lying? That there's collusion?" The lawyer appeared distressed rather than indignant.

"Not necessarily. Mr. Harmon could have made the call to his secretary and another call, too."

"Pure speculation."

"Detective Link saw him dial twice."

"I misdialed the first time. I had to start over."

Maynard smiled. "You'll have to do better, Lieutenant."

"If your client has nothing to hide, why doesn't he simply tell us where he was on the occasion in question?"

"But he has told you. He's made a clean breast of his peccadilloes."

"Let's not go over that same ground, Mr. Maynard. You know that we can trace his movements in Chicago. We can find out where he went and with whom and, having got that far, why—but at a cost of time and effort. He can save us those man-hours."

"Yes, yes, I've already explained all that." Maynard remained patient. "I've advised Mr. Harmon to be frank with you, purely in the spirit of cooperation, to do his duty as a citizen. However, he claims that to do so would prejudice his career." Alexander Maynard folded his pudgy hands across his belly in a gesture that said: *I'm a reasonable man, and I've done my best for both of you. The next move is up to you.*

Felix made it. "Book him, Sergeant."

Capretto took a step toward Harmon.

"Ah . . . one more minute, Lieutenant, if you don't mind, before we get into the paper work. It doesn't matter where my client was or what he was doing unless he was at the scene of one of your two homicides. Can you put him there? Otherwise, I'll have him out before Sergeant Capretto is through signing him in. You know that."

"I've got a witness who saw the killer enter Arabella Broome's building at the relevant time."

Maynard looked expectantly at his client.

"I wasn't there!" Harmon almost pleaded.

"Nevertheless . . ." Maynard waited, but Harmon would say no more. The lawyer sighed. "I'd appreciate a few minutes alone with my client, Lieutenant."

"Of course. No, no, stay here— we'll just step outside." Felix nodded to Joe, and the two of them walked into the hall.

Felix strolled to a window and looked out. "You know what I want most in the world right now?"

"A witness who could really place the killer at the scene."

"That would help. No, I was thinking how good a cigarette would taste. You know how long it's been since I gave it up? Well, there are still times when I get the most terrific yen for a drag."

Joe smiled feebly. The lieutenant's confidence only underscored his own qualms. "Lieutenant . . . the boy in the street outside the Broome residence, Ted Storch, he only got a glimpse of the repairman; he had no particular reason to notice him. He says himself that even if the man was wearing the uniform, he couldn't make an identification. Without the uniform . . ."

"Right. But neither Maynard nor Harmon knows that."

"Suppose they bluff it out?"

Felix formed his lips into a soundless whistle. "Risky—for them. We won't be any worse off than we are now."

The door opened and Maynard beckoned. "Mr. Harmon is innocent and is therefore not afraid of any confrontation."

*He's calling it,* Joe thought, *what lousy luck.*

"However," the lawyer continued, "witnesses have been known to make mistakes. Even a mistaken identification can be severely damaging, as we all know only too well. Therefore, Mr. Harmon has decided to divulge the name of the man with whom he met in Chicago. Naturally, since the meeting has no connection with the crimes, there would be no purpose in your making the information public."

Felix said nothing. He took his chair and waited for Harmon to speak; Cap struggled to conceal his elation.

Harmon began: "On the morning of the twenty-third I was in Chicago and I met with Gideon B. Speandex of Speandex Metals. I suppose you've heard of him?"

"I've also heard of Henry Ford."

Harmon glowered but remembered his situation. "Well, then you understand how it is."

"Frankly, no. Why all the secrecy?"

"I'm planning a move. Or I was. God knows . . ." He shifted direction. "Mr. Speandex is a tough negotiator. I'm after the presidency of one of his divisions. Naturally, there are other contenders. I more or less have to buy the job." In the face of Felix's determined blankness he had to finish. "With certain information."

"Concerning your present company. Now I understand." Felix said. "Well, business ethics aren't my line. If Mr. Speandex will confirm the time of the meeting. . . ."

"That's just it, he won't!" Harmon cried. "You see, the matter hasn't been finalized. My board hasn't given approval to the . . . project in question. If it learns that Speandex knows and is prepared to get on the market first, they'll switch to the alternate plan. Speandex won't like that. He won't care how it happened, just that I couldn't keep my mouth shut. He'll disavow the whole thing. He's not anxious to soil his reputation needlessly. My own people will figure where the leak came from, and I'll be out with both parties."

"I see. There are other ways of checking the meeting. If you'll tell me where it was held . . ."

"Along the shore of Lake Michigan. On a bench near the Field Museum."

"You're not making it easy."

Harmon glared at his lawyer. "I told you it wouldn't do any good."

"Don't give up, Mr. Harmon," Felix cut in. "We'll find somebody who saw you—park attendant, peanut vendor, nursemaid, stroller . . . I assume it was a fairly nice day, certainly not pouring rain, or you wouldn't have elected to stay outside."

"It was a nice day."

"Good. Now about your call last night. . . ."

"Don't you ever let up? All right, all right. The call was to Mr. Speandex to tell him the business was still undecided. That the board would come to a conclusion at its next meeting—a month from now."

"So. And the call to your secretary?"

"I did make two calls."

Felix didn't need to glance at Maynard to know he'd scored. He got up to indicate it was over. "We'll let you know the results of our inquiries in Chicago. Meanwhile, you'll stay in the city?"

"I haven't got anywhere else to go."

"Ah . . . one more question and you don't have to answer this one if you don't want to. To all appearances you're doing very well in your present position. Any extra salary or benefits Speandex could offer would probably be offset by taxes. Why are you so anxious to leave the company you now head?"

"My father-in-law is chairman of the board."

"I see."

"No, damn it, you don't!" Harmon exploded. He pulled himself straight. "My wife is an alcoholic. She stinks of it; it oozes out of every pore. I can't stand to be near her, and I want a divorce."


Felix tilted his chair back so that he could look straight up at the ceiling. He laced his fingers together and tapped his thumbs.

Neither Joe nor David Link spoke.

"That leaves us with the identikit man and Ellis," Felix said.

"Ellis was in his office the morning of the twenty-third," Joe pointed out.

Felix grunted. "That's about on par with Jerry Pepper's being in class, wouldn't you say?"

"Yes, sir."

"And how about that phone call he claims he was making when he got Officer Mulcahaney instead?"

The lieutenant was testy whenever Norah was mentioned. It puzzled Joe. Felix could usually find a redeeming trait in the most obnoxious officer under his command. Was he down on Norah just because she was a woman? "She hasn't called in yet," he replied.

Felix compressed his lips and pulled the phone over to dial. Joe was close enough so that he could hear the ring, twice, and the interruption of the third.

"So you're still there."

Not an auspicious beginning, Joe thought. He could visualize Norah's reaction—her sudden flush and the hurt bewilderment. He knew that under her dogged self-possession she was sensitive and very much in need of reassurance. Joe had decided that her aggressiveness was only a shield. The lieutenant was handling her all wrong.

"How about that number?" Felix asked in that coldly disapproving tone he'd recently adopted toward her. "You did? . . . What excuse did you make? . . . That's reasonable . . . . No!" he snapped suddenly. "If I'd wanted you to check it out, I would have said so. There are other people on the squad, Mulcahaney, and they all pull together—under my direction. We can't afford individual, uncoordinated, impulse effort. Just give me the number." He made a note on a pad. "So. See to it that you're out of there within the hour." He hung up.

Felix winced, sighed, then ripped the sheet off the pad and handed it to Cap. "Go ahead." He indicated the phone he'd just used himself.

Joe dialed, got the standard three rings, then a recorded announcement. "It's a nonoperating number," he told the lieutenant.

Felix pursed his lips into a silent whistle. "That takes care of Ellis' story about the girlfriend and the broken date. He sure thought fast, didn't he?"

"You want me to get the last subscriber's name and address?"

"I've got another job for you."

"Yes, sir."

"You, David, take over on Ellis. Find out what he was up to last night."

"Yes, *sir*." Link jumped.

"Wait a minute! Everybody's in such a hurry. Nobody needs instruction anymore."

David stopped and goggled. Joe looked at the floor.

"I don't want Ellis approached directly. Go to his building; ask around; find out whether he was in or out last night. Then go to his office. Talk to the women about him, but make sure he doesn't know you're doing it."

Now, besides being puzzled, David Link was a little miffed. He hadn't needed reminding. "I'll be careful, Lieutenant."

"And be back by"— as Felix checked his watch, the phone rang— "by seven. Well, all right, get going." He held off answering till the young detective was out of the office. "Felix here. . . . You did, eh? Good work. . . . No. . . ." He stared straight at Joe. "Cap's out, but as soon as he gets back, I'll send him over . . . Not at all, thank *you*." He hung up. "That was Safe and Loft. They've picked up a man who looks like your identikit picture. They got him last night for B and E. His MO is very interesting. He calls the intended victim by telephone and makes a date, and while she waits at the appointed place, he loots her apartment in comfort."

"That's a new one."

"I don't know. You could call it a variation of the theater ticket gambit. You heard what I told Safe and Loft?"

"Yes, Lieutenant."

"Well, wake up, Sergeant! If their B and E is the guy who shook you, he was booked four hours before Carmen Piñero was strangled. So. It looks like we've got to backtrack. Here's what I want you to do."

# Chapter 14

Norah got the telephone number the lieutenant wanted from Ellis and called it in right away. Felix thanked her but remained cool. She was deeply disappointed. She had reviewed with the strictest objectivity of which she was capable where she could possibly have gone wrong in the past few days, what word or action could have revealed to the killer that she was a decoy. In all honesty she didn't feel she was responsible. It was Norah's first taste of defeat through circumstance rather than personal fault.

The whole idea had been hers, of course, she'd volunteered, and the lieutenant had only reluctantly agreed. She was aware, though he hadn't said it, that what upset him was not even that the killer had made dupes of them all but that another woman had died. In her place? Maybe not. But the possibility that Carmen Piñero's death might have been avoided if police attention hadn't been riveted on Norah was a burden she couldn't easily shake off. If only to make amends for that, she would have been grateful to be able to stay on the case, working in the background on any kind of tedious job. She couldn't really blame the lieutenant for not wanting her.

One person had been pleased that she was off the case—her father. When she'd called to tell him she was coming home, he'd been jubilant. Henry would be relieved too when he heard. Well, might as well finish packing, she thought. The doorbell rang. Who could that be?

"Robert!"

"Hi." Ellis grinned at her surprise. "Well, aren't you going to ask me in?"

"Oh. I'm just getting ready to leave, Robert. Aren't you working today?"

"Lunch hour. Extended lunch hour, so I can help a friend move."

"That's nice of you, but you didn't need to bother."

"No bother."

He still smiled; but there was a difference, and it made her nervous. It made her realize suddenly that all the other tenants were away at their jobs and they were the only ones on the floor. Why should she be nervous with Robert? "I've only got a couple of suitcases. I was going to get a taxi."

"I'll be your porter. We can stop for a bite of lunch on the way. What's the matter, Norah? You expecting somebody else?"

She was instantly relieved. He was only jealous. It seemed her fate to get involved with jealous men. "Of course not," she reassured him.

"If you are expecting someone else, or if you'd rather go alone just say so."

"No. No, I told you." What else could she say? What else could she do but stand aside and let him in? "I'm glad you're here. I'm just finishing my packing."

He was instantly and touchingly pleased. "Can I help? Sit on a suitcase or something?"

She smiled in return. "No, but you can keep me company."

She let him follow her into the bedroom. There in that smaller area the uneasiness came back. She found his presence stifling. Why? She'd instinctively trusted Ellis, and he'd checked out clean. Suddenly Norah noticed that he was nervous too, just as nervous as she.

He lit a cigarette and took a stance blocking the doorway. Well, the room was tiny, the bed took up most of the space—where else could he stand?

"Why don't you bring a chair in from the living room?" She only wanted to get him out of that doorway. When he didn't answer, she turned over her shoulder to look at him. The window was at right angles so the light came from behind him, putting his face partly in shadow, but she could clearly read the doubt on it.

"Why have you got two telephones?"

Dumb, stupid, careless! She should never have let him into the bedroom. She had to think fast. "The black phone was here when I moved in. I asked for a colored phone, and they brought it but never got around to taking the old one out." She could only pray that the black phone (the police phone) wouldn't ring. She'd have a hard time explaining how it happened they were both working.

The thing to do was to finish her packing and get out. Quickly and methodically she set about opening and emptying drawers and transferring her neatly stacked clothing to one of the two suitcases open on the bed. "There." She slammed the cases shut. "All done."

"Aren't you going to check the closet?"

"I have."

"Pays to be sure. Here, let me." Putting out his cigarette in the ashtray on the bureau, Ellis reached past her. Involuntarily Norah flinched.

"What's the matter? Why are you do edgy?"

"I'm not edgy."

"Well, look at that. You were going to forget your purse."

She laughed as easily as she could. "You're right, I was." She reached.

They collided. The purse fell from the closet shelf to the floor, spilling its contents. They both stared down in silence at the gun and shield.

Finally, after a very long time Ellis spoke. "They are yours?" All she could do was nod.

It seemed difficult for him to take it in. "You said you worked in TV. Those stories in the papers . . . about your husband . . . about how he took an overdose of sleeping pills . . . all lies, a trap." Neither of them noticed that he was now admitting having seen those stories. "And I fell for it! I sure fell for it. That is until today, until you asked me for that telephone number." Slowly he shook his head. "Even then, you know, I argued with myself. I wanted to believe in you. You don't think I swallowed that bit about your father wanting to check up on me, do you?"

"My father did want to."

He snorted. "Tell your 'father' not to bother to call the number. I didn't give you the right one. I'm not that much of a fool. To tell you the truth, I felt uncomfortable about you at the beginning—you played it too straitlaced for a pickup and at the same time you were real eager. I should have trusted my instincts."

"I wish you hadn't given me the wrong number, Robert." The worst was over, Norah thought with relief. She'd about recovered from the shock of having her identity discovered, and Robert, in spite of his recriminations, seemed to be adjusting to it too. As long as they were able to talk about it . . . She tried to sound calm and reasonable. "Please give me the right number, Robert. It's for your protection."

"Is it? You don't say! Well, thanks just the same, but I don't buy that. Anyhow, I know how to protect myself."

"None of this has anything to do with you." Norah gestured to indicate the apartment. "Believe me. You've been eliminated. I mean it, Robert. You have been eliminated." She licked her lips nervously. The gun still lay on the floor between them. She must pick it up before he did. If she could divert his attention for even a moment. . . . "The case is closed. Why else would I be moving out? And I'm letting you take me home. I wouldn't do that if you were involved."

He was wavering, but his eyes remained fixed on her face. "Would I let you come in here while I'm alone if you were still a suspect? You can see we're alone?"

His glance shifted then, for the merest fraction. Norah stooped instantly and reached for the gun. He bent too, his hand closing on her wrist and wrenching it from her.

The doorbell rang.

It paralyzed them both. Each stared at the other, not knowing what to do. Ellis, gun in hand, recovered first.

"Don't make a sound," he whispered, "not a sound." He

grabbed her arm and, pulling her along with him, made for the open window, all the while keeping her own gun on her. He sat on the window ledge and swung his legs over to the fire escape. Then he pulled her hand over the sill. Was he going to try to take her along? Before she could decide how much resistance she could put up, he had brought the window down on her wrist and was speeding up the metal stairs toward the roof.

It hurt, but she was too surprised to scream. The pain kept her from moving for several seconds. Then she had to raise the window with her free hand to release herself before she could even look out. He was gone, of course. By now he'd have run to another roof and was probably coming down through another building. She couldn't give chase without her gun, and shouting an alarm was useless.

Meanwhile, the doorbell was ringing insistently.

"All right, all right, I'm coming."

There was nothing for it but to call in and report, admit that she'd let Ellis break her cover and that he'd bolted. What a mess!

"Norah? Norah! Are you there?"

Henry! It was Henry at the door. Now what? If there was one thing she didn't need right now, it was Henry in full spate. He was pounding on the door, and if she didn't open it, he was capable of breaking it down. "Coming."

Henry was pale. His dark eyes blazed. "What took you so long?"

"I . . . ah. . . ." She hesitated. She was still breathing hard and he was sure to notice her agitation: Henry never missed her slightest reaction. She just couldn't go through the whole sequence with him right that minute. He'd rant about the risks she was taking, nag at her to resign, and the bickering routine would start all over again. "I had to put my dress on."

"I thought I heard voices."

"No." She denied it flatly; she wasn't even up to concocting a reasonable explanation like the radio being on. Let him take it or leave it. She turned her back on him and headed for the bedroom. "Excuse me, I have to call in." She shut the door.

Neither the lieutenant nor Joe was available. They said Joe was out of town—odd because this was the second time she'd tried and couldn't reach him. Anyhow, she got David Link. In a way it made it easier—especially the part about having her own gun used against her.

Link was kind, too kind, making excuses for her because she was a woman. He didn't say that; he didn't need to; it was in every soothing syllable. "Now, don't worry, Norah, I'll get the ball rolling on Ellis. You go on home like the lieutenant told you."

None of them trusted her! She stood for a moment with her hand over her forehead and eyes. Then she remembered Henry. She opened the bedroom door.

For once in his life Henry didn't press her with questions. "Your father says you're coming home."

"That's right."

"Norah . . . I'm sorry. I'm sorry the stakeout, or whatever you call it, didn't work. I really am."

She was startled. "How do you know it didn't work?"

"Well, if there'd been any kind of big arrest it would have been in the papers. And you certainly would have told your father. And you wouldn't look like you do."

The unexpectedness of his sympathy, plus reaction from the encounter with Ellis and the subsequent talk with Link and his excessively gentle handling, was too much. Her eyes filled; her voice shook. "I did my best." She was referring to the last fiasco with Ellis, though Henry couldn't know that.

"Of course you did."

He went to her and tentatively put an arm around her. It felt good. There was a lot to be said for a good steady man, not exciting maybe, but reliable, comforting, there when you needed him. That was Henry all right. She hoped he wouldn't spoil it by asking her to quit the job, not at this moment. God knew she felt like quitting; maybe she would, too, but without being prodded.

"Sweetheart." He was encouraged to hold her closer. "I'm sorry you're disappointed, but I can't help being glad you're coming home."

The passion of his kiss surprised her. It left her gasping. The next surprise was that she wasn't sure she liked it. She'd wanted fervor from him, and now here she was resisting it.

He wouldn't let her go. "Marry me, Norah, marry me. I want you. I need you." His voice rose, cracked with emotion.

She couldn't help being touched by this uncharacteristic intensity.

"I realize we've only known each other a short time, and I've tried to be patient . . ."

Had he really been holding back while she'd chafed over his patience?

"But if we know we love each other, then time doesn't really enter into it, does it? I can't wait any longer." He was kissing her again, his hands groping. "Marry me, Norah, say you'll marry me."

She'd put her hopes on Ellis, but her womanly intuition of his innocence had proved wrong. So she was left with Henry as she'd somehow known she would be—good, steady, and suddenly very ardent Henry.

"Yes," Norah said.

He released her instantly and stared. "You mean it?"

"Yes. Yes, I do."

Nothing was happening as it should, or rather as she had imagined it would. Instead of now sweeping her up again, he fell back even farther in a kind of abject gratitude. "You've made me so happy. I can't believe it. And I'll make you happy, oh, I will, I will."

"I know that, Henry."

"You'll never regret it, sweetheart, I promise you. You'll never regret it. Well, come on, let's go home and tell your father the good news."

"Yes, let's."

It was only as she was giving the place a final check before locking up that Norah noticed the stub of Ellis' cigarette in the bedroom ashtray. She couldn't explain about Ellis to Henry now, not after she'd so flatly denied that anyone had been in the apartment. She could say the sergeant had left it earlier. Henry had met Joe and knew he was "carrying." Did he also know that Joe didn't smoke? Better not take the chance. Anyway, Henry hadn't noticed the cigarette because Henry, being Henry, would never have been able to keep still about it.

Henry wasn't much of a talker while driving, and Norah had plenty to brood about during the short ride home. Of course, she could hardly expect to be jubilant after the mess of her assignment and the way she'd let Ellis escape. Still she shouldn't be feeling this depressed and hopeless after just getting engaged. She'd always imagined that when she finally made the decision to get married, all her cares would drop away. Instead, she now felt as though she'd just closed the door on her future. On the other hand, she'd be willing to bet that plenty of girls reacted the same way when making the irrevocable commitment but were ashamed to admit it. It was just a question of getting used to the idea that marriage was a beginning, not an end. Meantime, it was almost easier to think about Ellis.

What would his next move be? He must know that she'd reported what had happened and the police would be on the lookout for him. Would he make a run for it? Would he risk going back to his apartment for clothes and money? Or would he stay and brazen it out? That would depend on how solid his alibis were. They had stood up once; would they again under closer scrutiny?

With a start, Norah realized they had arrived. Henry had parked and was getting out.

She gave him a vague smile as he took the suitcases out of the back and carried them across the sidewalk and into the building; then she went on with the problem of Ellis. She wasn't afraid of him, not anymore. If he harmed her now, it was as good as admitting his guilt. Anyhow, how could he find her?

Where had Henry gone to? Evidently he'd decided to take the bags directly upstairs. Meantime, Norah got out of the car.

When she returned, Henry was standing on the sidewalk, waiting. "Where did you disappear to?"

"I went down the street to make a phone call."

"Another one?"

"I suddenly realized I hadn't left a forwarding address."

"Who's going to need your forwarding address?"

That was a slip, a bad one, arousing his instant jealous suspicion. "The dry cleaner."

"Oh. Couldn't you have waited another two minutes and used your own phone?"

"Yes, of course . . . I just . . . wanted to be sure not to miss him. I'm sorry if I kept you waiting. Don't be annoyed."

"I'm not, only . . . oh, hell, Norah! Why did you think I asked you to sit in the car while I took the bags up?" He pointed to the fire hydrant. "Your going off like that could have cost me a fifteen-dollar ticket."

# Chapter 15

"He's handsome, a good dresser, has a promising job, and doesn't drink—in other words he's eminently eligible, but he hasn't given the office talent a tumble." Link was summing up the results of his recent interviews regarding Robert Ellis, comparing them with what had already been learned about him, looking for any small thing that might have been missed.

"You're the expert, Cap, how do you explain that?" Felix asked.

Just back from a second trip out of town on the lieutenant's orders, Joe was too worried about what he had learned to engage in banter. He was surprised to find the lieutenant indulging in it.

"They romanticize Ellis," Link went on. "Seems he was badly wounded in Vietnam, recovered enough to be able to resume a normal life, and was all set to marry his childhood sweetheart. Two days before the wedding the girl killed herself."

Felix sat up. "Why?"

"She discovered she had terminal cancer."

"Is that true?"

"They believe it."

Felix sighed. "How about his alibi for the twenty-third? Does it still stand?"

"I couldn't find anyone who saw Ellis leave the building. On the other hand, the way Barlow, Borden, and Dunbar is laid out—executive on the twentieth floor, art on the eleventh, promotion on the fifteenth—he'd have a hard time proving where he was every minute of that morning."

"How about an alibi for last night, for the Piñero homicide?"

Link shook his head. "Got in around eleven p.m., made a point of mentioning to the doorman how lousy the movie had been. The doorman goes off at twelve."

"So. We don't know any more than we did before," Felix grunted. "Okay, David, that's all for now; write it up." When Link was gone, Felix leaned back in his swivel chair and regarded Capretto thoughtfully. "Ellis has admitted to Mulcahaney that the number he gave her isn't the one he was calling the night he got her instead. He refused to give her the right number."

Joe thought about it. "Could be we were wrong about the girlfriend, could be there's been one all along, but he doesn't want Norah to know." He admitted to himself that he was bending over backward in Ellis' behalf because he didn't want to be influenced by Norah's obvious interest in Ellis—which was just as bad as trying to pin it on him. "Doesn't feel right, though," he added honestly.

"Because it isn't. He went up to the apartment at lunchtime today and found Mulcahaney's gun and shield."

"God!" Joe's handsome face darkened.

"He held her own gun on her to make his getaway."

"He could have killed her right then and there!"

"The doorbell rang."

"Oh, God."

"He won't go after her now. What would be the point?"

"Maybe revenge is more important to him than caution."

"I doubt it."

How could the lieutenant be so casual? Joe was honestly perplexed by Felix's entire attitude toward Norah. "Sir, we can't take the chance."

"He doesn't know her real name or where she lives." Felix dismissed the matter. "Relax."

What the hell? What the hell! Joe was prepared to make an issue. "Lieutenant, she's entitled to protection."

"Did I say she wasn't going to get it?" Felix snapped. "Damn it, Joe, keep your shirt on." Felix flipped the switch on the intercom. "Brennan, call the DA for a search warrant for Robert Ellis' place, then come on in." He motioned for Joe to sit down again. "Now, here's what we're going to do."

Norah was finishing the dinner dishes while her father in the living room read the sports pages; soon he'd put on television. The kitchen window being directly over the sink Norah could look out on Eighty-fourth Street, then diagonally past the corner to Riverside Drive and get a wedgelike view of the Hudson and the Palisades on the other side. The night was dark—no moon, no stars—lit only in flashes by the commercial electric signs on the Jersey shore. Rain was predicted. The city waited, hot and still.

Norah had given the super at her old building a telephone number instead of a forwarding address. The telephone was the killer's weapon, and Norah wanted him to use it again. She was still shaken by the encounter with Ellis, still found it hard to believe that he was the psychotic killer they were after. The point was now that he'd lost his anonymity would he call again? Could he resist?

He couldn't. Robert Ellis called not half an hour after she got home. He was nervous; his voice shook; he stuttered and stumbled and repeated himself. He begged her to forgive him if he'd hurt her. He'd panicked; he wanted to explain why, he wanted to confess. . . . He needed help; he begged Norah to help him. He was almost incoherent.

Obviously he was sick, very sick. Norah almost felt sorry for him, except that the memory of Arabella Broome and Vicky Neumann and Ruth Emerson was too clear. It was he who urged the meeting, though, pleaded for it, promising to turn himself in if she were not satisfied with his explanation, offering to make no trouble if she decided to take him in herself.

His eagerness and abjectness made her wary. It was what she'd been after when she'd made it possible for him to reach her, of course. She suggested they meet at The Bulldog. It was nearby, and since it was an English pub type of saloon, there'd naturally be no risk of a chance encounter with her father. It bothered her a little that Ellis offered no objection to such a public place. He made her promise, of course, that she'd come alone. . . .

Norah called the lieutenant right away. She'd learned by now that playing a lone hand was for amateurs and fools. She also knew perfectly well that she shouldn't have set the meet up without consulting Felix first. She was prepared for a curt reprimand, but evidently the lieutenant no longer had enough interest in her to bother even with that. He did agree to stake out the bar, though with a marked lack of enthusiasm. Of course, it was a routine matter to him.

So the entire area around The Bulldog would be swarming with men, inside and out, and she'd be absolutely safe. Then why did the dishes keep slipping out of her hands? She was just putting away the serving platter when she noticed that a couple of grains of rice still stuck to it. She turned the tap back on and reached for the soap. . . .

Crash.

"What's the matter?" Her father called out from the next room.

She didn't answer right away, and the next thing she knew he was there, having come as close to a run as his dragging foot would permit, looking white and anxious out of all proportion.

"I broke the platter." She tried to sound offhand, but it came out querulous.

"Oh." Patrick Mulcahaney stared from his daughter to the fragments on the floor and back again. "Well, there's no need to get frazzled. It's the cheap set."

"I'm not frazzled," she retorted testily.

He took no notice of her tone. "That's okay then." He shrugged and started back. "Don't cut yourself cleaning up."

Well now, that was odd. He'd watched her closely all through dinner, and she knew she hadn't been able to hide her nervousness, yet he'd neither commented nor pried —which was not like Patrick Mulcahaney. And now at this positive indication that something was wrong—why, he turned his back and walked away! It was almost as though he didn't want to acknowledge that anything was wrong for fear of finding out what. And that was completely out of character. Probably he attributed her state of excitement to the engagement. Maybe he even sensed she had second thoughts about it, and he didn't want to add importance to them by discussing them.

Let it go at that.

She got out the dustpan and broom and swept up the debris. They'd had roast lamb for dinner, so the oven could use a spray cleaning. When that was finished and she couldn't think of anything else to do, it was still only a quarter of eight. The meet was for nine. She hadn't decided yet what kind of excuse she'd give her father for going out. If she admitted it was police business, he'd ask a lot of questions. A date with Henry would be much more acceptable—only how to explain why Henry wasn't calling for her?

While she was trying to resolve it, the doorbell rang. Again her father moved with unaccustomed briskness to answer it. She heard his hearty exclamation.

"Henry! What a nice surprise! Norah didn't say you were coming over."

Oh, no! she thought, oh, no. . . . Now how was she going to get rid of Henry? If she pleaded an assignment to Henry, he'd insist on driving her wherever she was going. The first thing to do was to stop him from settling down with Dad in front of the TV. Was there a ball game on tonight? With the pennant race nearing its end there was bound to be. Oh, damn.

"Norah!" Her father calling.

"Coming." Damn.

Henry was standing in the middle of the room with a bunch of white chrysanthemums and an apologetic smile.

"I know we didn't have a date, but I just had to see you. I won't stay long."

That brought enough relief so that she could smile back. "These are lovely, Henry, thanks. I'll get a vase."

"No need for you to rush off, my boy." Her father was at his most expansive. "You and Norah have lots to talk about, plans to make, all that. Anyhow, I have to go out. So you stay and keep Norah from getting lonely."

"Dad!" He was at it again, being tactful, pushing them at each other. Well, they were engaged, weren't they? Naturally, her father assumed he was doing them a favor. She tried not to show her irritation. "Where are you going?"

"Well now. . . ." Her father smiled, both sly and sheepish. "They're after me to be district leader again."

"You didn't agree?"

"Why not? You're a grown woman now. You have a job and . . . a man. I shouldn't have to baby-sit you anymore."

She couldn't hide her dismay, though she did try to hide the hurt. "I didn't know you felt like that."

"I tried to tell you."

"Yes. Yes, I suppose you did."

"No need to take on about it. Now that you and Henry have finally made up your minds . . . well, you'll be glad the old man has something to occupy him—until the little ones come along naturally."

As close to smirking as Norah had ever seen him, Patrick Mulcahaney got his raincoat out of the hall closet while she and Henry stood and watched, tongue-tied. When he was ready, her father paused; unexpectedly he came back and, cradling her face in his still-lumpy workman's hands, gave her a resounding kiss. "Don't wait up for me, children."

When he was gone, Norah heaved a sigh, then managed a rueful smile at Henry. "I didn't know I was the one holding him back. I thought . . . well, I'll put the flowers in water. Want some coffee?"

"All right."

She didn't waste time over the flowers, stuffing them into the vase any which way, nor in setting out the coffee on a tray along with the brownies she'd bought during the afternoon's marketing. The time that had dragged was now rushing relentlessly by. Eight thirty-five, and she had planned to leave for the rendezvous at quarter of nine. She served the coffee.

"As a matter of fact, Henry, I will ask you not to stay. I don't feel awfully well. I was planning to go to bed early. Do you mind?"

"What's wrong?"

She couldn't tell him that she was taking part in a stakeout. He'd only fuss about the risk; they'd quarrel over it. Besides, she had no right to tell him. "Nothing. I mean, nothing serious. It's . . . well, you know, the time of the month." She was terribly embarrassed; she hoped Henry would be too.

"Oh. Oh. Is there anything I can get for you at the drugstore?"

"No, thanks. I think if I just lie down . . ."

"Yeah, sure." He didn't get up to leave, though. He just kept sitting on the sofa and looking at her. "Norah, you're not angry because I came up unexpectedly tonight?"

"No. Whatever gave you that idea?" What had?

"You didn't have other plans . . . or anything?"

"What plans? Oh, Henry!"

"I'm sorry. I don't mean to doubt your word only . . . you didn't seem very glad to see me. I'm jealous. All right, I admit it. I can't help it. I know I've no reason. I know you're the most straightforward, honest girl in the world. It's why I love you. It's why I've been patiently waiting for you to make up your mind. I knew you weren't teasing me, that your uncertainty was sincere, that once you'd resolved it and made up your mind, you'd stick with your decision. You are going to stick with it, Norah, aren't you?"

"Of course. Who said I wasn't?"

"Then if you mean it, let's not wait, let's get married right away. We can go for the blood tests tomorrow and get the license and be married this weekend."

"This weekend?"

"Why not? Why not, Norah, if you're sure?"

His doubt was in the open—it had sucked the juices out of him and left him withered and old. Norah had a vision of

Henry as he would be in his old age, and she was revolted. At the same time she felt sorry for him and responsible and extremely nervous. He'd succeeded in making her feel guilty about the meet with Ellis. Or rather that she was going behind his back. But if she told him about it now, he wouldn't believe it was the job and not personal. Besides, she couldn't tell him. How could she even consider telling him? It was absolutely impossible.

"I can't be ready this weekend, Henry. There are things I have to do. I have to go shopping—I need clothes, a trousseau...."

"We can get whatever you need later."

"I'd like a nice wedding, not fancy, but nice. With all our friends there. A girl only gets married once." She was still trying to temporize.

"You don't want to."

"I didn't say that."

"It's what you mean."

"All right then. I don't want to. Not this weekend."

Now he got up. "Or ever?"

"I didn't say that. Don't make me say it."

They glared at each other; then, and as in so many instances before, Henry backed down.

"I'll call you in the morning. I hope you feel better." Stiffly, he strode to the door. "Be sure to put the chain back on after I leave."

Now Norah felt worse than ever. Though she'd managed to put Henry in the wrong, she couldn't really blame him. He'd sensed her impatience for him to be gone, so, as a newly engaged man, what could he think? Maybe in the morning it would be all right to tell him what she'd been up to, if the lieutenant gave permission. Meantime ... she looked at her watch. Nine! She was supposed to be there! She couldn't rush right over because she had to allow time for Henry to drive away. It wouldn't do for him to see her. All right, say five minutes for Henry to get away, five for her to walk over...

She put on her raincoat and checked the miniature tape recorder in the pocket with which the lieutenant had provided her. The idea was to get an admission of guilt from Ellis. The tape recorder was a backup in case their conversation couldn't be clearly overheard by the police witnesses. Now... it was safe to go. It had to be.

The hall and elevator were empty, as was the lobby. Norah had the eerie sensation of being alone in the building. Outside, the first wisps of fog were creeping up the empty street. She felt the need to be among people, but turning the corner to Riverside Drive, she saw that it too was deserted. The fog rose up from the shores of the Hudson like a silent enemy. The traffic lights winked uselessly in the near absence of cars. Even the dog walkers had given up.

The amber lights of The Bulldog were directly ahead. Norah had been there once or twice with Artie; it was a cozy place, with dark paneling, shaded lights, and a dart board. A safe place, Norah assured herself as she walked briskly toward it, at the same time casting a quick and, she hoped, casual look around. She couldn't spot any of the men on the stakeout, but then she wasn't supposed to. She opened the door to the accompaniment of an old-fashioned tinkling bell overhead and entered confidently. Only the bartender looked up.

Joe Capretto, slouched at the near end of the bar, didn't react, nor did Roy Brennan at a table halfway down toward the back. But they knew she was there, of course. She didn't at the moment recognize anyone else.

"Can I help you, miss?"

The bartender was a big bruiser with the typical saloon pallor. Was that scowl of disapproval permanently etched, or had he put it on specifically for her? "I'm looking for someone; I guess he's not here yet. I'll wait."

The bartender shrugged but kept his eyes on her with open suspicion as she headed toward a rear booth. What did he take her for—a hooker? Norah sat down and ordered a beer.

Time passed. The door opened and shut, and the bell above it tinkled, and Norah craned out into the aisle to see; but it was never Ellis. She looked anxiously at her watch. Only twenty after nine. Still, he should have been here by now . . . if he was coming. Then the surly bartender was standing over her.

"Your name Norah? Phone call."

What had gone wrong? Had he been delayed? Or—Norah's stomach knotted painfully—did he sense a trap? She entered the booth and picked up the receiver cord. "This is Norah."

"You dirty, filthy, lying cheat."

The voice was low, harsh, guttural, and vicious with hate . . . the voice of the caller.

"You broke faith, Norah. I trusted you and you deceived me."

The worst had happened—he'd spotted the stakeout! She couldn't lose him, not now, not when they had come so close. "No, no, I didn't. I'm here alone. I swear it."

"You expect me to believe that? You think I don't know what you did in that apartment? I watched while the man went in and out. Which one are you drinking and carousing with now, huh? Which one? You whore."

He pronounced it "hoore," and somehow that made it even nastier. Norah winced, but it was only the beginning of the abuse and curses he poured out on her. It was horrible, worse than she could possibly have anticipated. She wanted to drop the receiver and run out of the booth straight to Joe; she wanted Joe to hold her while she cried with shame and revulsion, but of course she couldn't. She had to stay . . . and listen . . . to the slime of his diseased imaginings as he worked himself into a slobbering frenzy. . . .

Finally, he was depleted; the vituperativeness became a repetitive mumble, and she managed to break in. "Please, please, it's not the way you think. Please come over here and let me explain."

The laugh began as a muffled, wretched cackle but grew into a renewed outburst of manic rage. "Do you think I'm a fool? Do you think I don't know that if I set foot in that place, I'm finished? You'll have your police friends waiting to truss me up and put me in a cage like an animal. But it'll never happen, never."

"Nobody will touch you, I swear. I promise." She sought frantically for some means to convince him. "Please, how can I make you believe me?"

There was a silence. A long one. Had he gone? Had he simply left her holding the open line?

"How can I be sure?"

Norah sensed the slyness, but she was too relieved that she hadn't lost him to take the time to analyze the reason for it. "What do you want me to do? I'll do whatever you say."

"If you're really sincere you'll meet me where I want, a place of my choosing, Norah. A place where I know we'll be alone."

She didn't hesitate. "Yes, all right, wherever you say."

"Down by the river then. There's a staircase at Eighty-sixth. You know it. I'll be at the bottom of the stairs. Leave now."

This time she heard the click as he hung up, and there was no question but that he was gone; then she too hung up slowly. Would he have come to the bar if there hadn't been a stakeout? Or had he planned it this way from the beginning? Of course, if he'd been smart enough to see through the apartment setup, how could they have thought he'd be fooled by this obvious trap? He'd only been stringing her along, playing on her nerves. There was something else, something she was missing....

Norah left the booth and went directly to Joe at the bar.

One look at her pale face, and he understood. "Was it bad?"

She nodded. "He wants me to meet him down by the river."

His reaction was instant. "You're not going."

"Right away," Norah added as though he hadn't spoken.

Joe beckoned to Brennan. "He wants her to go down to the river. We can't protect you down there, Norah."

"We'll lose the whole case if I don't go."

There was no trace of the old Norah's girlish defiance; in its place was quiet determination. The experience had shaken her, naturally, Joe thought. He took her hands in his and held them. "That's better than losing you."

But Norah only smiled wanly—she was struggling with a new possibility, a terrible, dreadful alternative. The more she thought about it, the surer she was that she'd finally stumbled on the truth. "He's going to get me, Joe, sooner or later. He's made up his mind. Let it be now."

Joe was very still. "What makes you think so?"

"It wasn't Ellis on the phone."

Joe glanced quickly toward Brennan, and Roy shook his head. "How can you be sure? We decided a long time ago that he was using some means to disguise his voice."

"He's still disguising it, but it's not Ellis."

"It has to be, Norah. How else do you explain his taking your gun and running?"

"I don't know. I don't know what Robert's done, what kind of trouble he's in, but he's not the man we're after."

"All the more reason for you not to go."

"I don't see it that way." Some of her normal cockiness was returning.

"If she could stall awhile . . ." Roy Brennan offered thoughtfully. "If she could give us enough time to get down there ahead of her. . . ."

"No!" Joe snapped. "Absolutely not."

Norah was surprised; it wasn't like Joe to be so curt.

Roy didn't take offense; he went on in the same mild, reasonable, objective manner. "If he spotted Norah, then the lieutenant's spotted him and has a tail on him. The tail is going to be down there by the river for sure."

Joe wavered. "Not for sure."

"In all probability, then. Will you accept it as a strong probability, Joe?"

"I'm not going to risk Norah's life on a strong probability."

Norah's chin came up, but she tried to be as reasonable as Brennan. "You and Roy will certainly be there and whoever else you've got deployed outside, right?"

Joe sighed.

"That's good enough for me." She smiled at both of them.

"We could be moving into position." Still quiet, Roy kept up the pressure.

"I know, I know. . . ."

"Joe, if I don't go now, I'll never feel safe again. Joe, I am going."

"All right, all right! But you listen to me, Norah Mulcahaney, and you follow my instructions. You're to wait here for fifteen minutes; I said fifteen, not one second less. By that time we'll have found cover in the area. I hope. I suppose the fog will help us as much as it will him. And you stay close to the foot of the stairs. Don't wander. For God's sake don't wander whatever you do."

"I understand."

"No bright ideas, Norah. Just follow orders."

"Yes, Sergeant, I promise."

"Yeah." Joe sighed. "Okay, Roy, let's go."

Now that she was alone, Norah didn't have to hide her nervousness.

"Miss? Why don't you sit over here? I'll see to it that nobody disturbs you." The bartender, evidently trying to make amends for his earlier surliness, waved at a stool in the corner beside the cash register.

Norah accepted the half-hidden seat gratefully and watched the blinking Schlitz clock over the bar. The hands moved very slowly; but in the end the minutes had passed too quickly, and she found she wasn't so eager after all. In fact, she was afraid. Again she thought of Arabella Broome. Arabella had been terrified, but she hadn't let that stop her—and Arabella hadn't had the protection Norah would have with Joe and Roy and the other men around her. She got off the stool and smiled a good-bye to her new friend.

The bartender waved and smiled back, but his face wasn't used to it.

Outside, the fog had thickened; it lay in turgid, soggy layers. Norah could feel its slimy suckers attaching to every exposed part of her flesh, then seeping through her coat —instant mold. It had obliterated the opposite shore, completely wiping out the Jersey lights. On this side there was still limited visibility—at least up here on the bluffs. She could make out the row of nineteenth-century globe lamps that marked the edge of the descent to the strip of park at the river's edge. Tatters of greenish vapor dripped from them. Beyond, the fog rose like a prison wall. What it would be like down below Norah didn't even want to think about.

The milky globes cast a platform of light that floated in the mist. Stepping up to the stair platform, she knew for those few moments it would take her to cross and start down she would be completely exposed. Not Joe or the men of the stakeout or the lieutenant himself, if he were there, would be able to protect her. But there would be little satisfaction for the caller to shoot her down; it wasn't his way. He'd want to talk to her some more first, taunt her, degrade and debase her. . . . That was almost a worse ordeal, she thought, and walked fast till she was in the dark again, the blessed safe dark, descending into a well of darkness and fog.

She had to guide herself by the handrail because after the first few steps she couldn't see at all. Though she was careful, probing each tread before putting her weight on it, the ground came up at her with an unexpected jolt that buckled her knees and jarred her spine. She gasped, then stood absolutely still.

"Hello?" she called tentatively.

If she couldn't see him, then he couldn't see her, and the men on the stakeout couldn't see either of them.

"Hello! Are you there?" She called out louder.

There was no answer. The fog had changed character; it was now a sponge that absorbed her voice. She moved with the tentative shuffle of the blind. Probably he would be at the rear, tucked under the sheltering stairway arch. She made a tight left turn in that direction. There was some kind of metal footrail. She had to stand away from the stair wall to clear it.

"This is Norah. Where are you?" Norah caught herself flinching at the hollowness of her own voice, at the strangeness of it. Was that a footstep? Was that someone breathing? "Here I am. Over here."

No answer this time either, and the footstep, if it had been a footstep, was not heard again. Hands out in front, she groped her way a half turn that should bring her back to the foot of the stairs. She edged her toes out, feeling for the low railing. It wasn't there. Had she turned in the wrong direction? She made a circle the other way, put out her foot again in the futile probe. Oh, Lord, she'd completely lost her bearings; she had no idea which way she was facing—toward the stair or toward the river! She had no idea how far she'd wandered.

Had she gone beyond the area of the stakeout?

Her aimless wandering was making it worse. She must stand still and wait for him to find her. There would sooner or later be gaps in the fog. She hoped Joe and the others would then locate her. Listening intently, Norah thought she could hear gentle lapping of water. Then . . . was that a small stone kicked along the cement walk?

She spoke loudly so that everyone could hear. "Is that you?" She turned in the direction of the sound.

As she did, hands reached out from behind and grabbed her by the throat with such force that she felt her handbag slide from her grip—and with it the substitute gun.

The hands were cold and strong. The thumbs anchored firmly at the back of her skull, and the fingers pressed against her larynx—but not so hard she couldn't breathe—and tight —but not so tight she couldn't have screamed. She didn't scream because she knew it would be the last sound of her life.

Any effort to try to loosen his grip would only result, she felt sure, in causing him to tighten it. She didn't even dare to reach into the pocket to turn on the tape recorder which she should have done as soon as she came down and hadn't because she'd been afraid of running out of tape—another mistake on the long, long list. Were they as close to the water's edge as the sounds indicated? If so, they were beyond earshot of the detectives, and the confrontation would be useless. She must make some kind of signal.

"Please...." She grunted as loud as the grip would allow, and the instant tightening of the grip warned her it could not be that loud again. It also brought a wave of nausea, and it was several seconds before she could overcome it enough to speak. "It's no use. You're trapped. The police are here. They're all around us."

He gave an extra jerk that pulled her back against him so that she could feel the spasm pass through his whole body. Then he relaxed. "You're lying again."

The voice was low, guttural, and still unrecognizable.

"No, no, I swear it."

"Then why don't they come out? Why don't they come out and get me? You see how futile your lies are. I want you to admit your lies, all of them. Cleanse yourself. Confess."

His grip was now so tight that Norah was having trouble just breathing. Her throat ached; the words scraped the raw membranes. "What . . . do you . . . want . . . me to say?"

"I want you to confess. Confess. Everything. Confess what you did in that apartment!"

For a moment Norah was honestly puzzled. "What I did in the apartment. . . . I don't understand." It hurt too much to go on protesting.

"Don't play dumb. Don't pretend innocence. You're a bitch, a filthy, fornicating bitch. You're like all the rest of them. A man was with you in that apartment last night. Alone with you. All night. I know. I saw him go in, and I saw the two of you come out."

Joe! He'd seen Joe.

"Don't tell me you just sat and talked!" the voice sneered, snarling, and leering, and hissing in her ear, yet sounding terribly distant. Was that the effect of fog, or was she on the verge of fainting for lack of air?

He gave her a brief, vicious shake as though he didn't want her fainting, not yet. "You have to be punished. You understand that?"

She couldn't make a sound. He had to ease his grip for her to make some kind of intelligible response.

"I . . . I . . . didn't do . . . anything wrong."

"Stop lying!" he hissed. "You want to die with the sin still on you?"

Now she understood, and she was terrified. "What . . . do you want?"

"I want you to confess."

"All right."

"Go on." He shook her impatiently.

Details? Was it details he was after? She was appalled. "I . . . I can't . . . I'm sorry. I am. I repent." Then she had an inspiration. "I'm too ashamed. Please. . . ." She began to whine sensing that it fed his ego. "Please . . . forgive me."

"It's not that easy. You have to earn forgiveness. You have to make atonement."

It was all clear now. "Like the others?" she murmured.

"Yes."

Norah thought she could detect the slightest note of regret. "You aren't any different. You're a disappointment to me, Norah. I thought you were different, but I was wrong. I thought you were decent and clean. You can be clean again—that's the main thing." He said it as though a new idea had struck him. "You can be washed clean!" Now he was more excited than angry.

His grip on her throat tightened again, and he yanked so abruptly she had to go along, half dragged by him and half assisting so as to ease the terrible strain. "Where are we . . . going?"

"Why, to wash you clean." He sounded very pleased indeed.

And suddenly Norah knew why—he meant to drown her in the river! Here in the center of this steel and stone city she was to die by drowning! "No. . . ." She held back, and the pressure on her throat made the single syllable an unintelligible gurgle.

"It's better if you go willingly, believe me." He was almost coaxing. "There's more merit in it if you do it yourself. But if you won't, I'll have to do it for you. There is no escape from just retribution."

No, Norah thought at the edge of despair, there isn't. The lieutenant and the others had surely lost her or by now they would have moved in. By now surely they'd heard enough—if they were around to hear. Even if the killer were suddenly to let her go, Norah doubted that her abused throat could manage any sounds loud enough to alert them—recognizable sounds, that is.

There was one last thing she must do so that when her body was found, if it was ever recovered from the dark waters, there would be evidence to save some other hapless victim. She pulled her lips back; her tongue felt thick; the pain of trying to speak was now almost beyond bearing—at the same time the pain was what kept her conscious.

"What did you say?"

All she could produce was a series of gasps—they would at least cover the click of the switch and the whir of the spools. She tried again. "R-r-ruth . . ."

He seemed to understand, or else he wanted to talk about it—a little of each probably. "Ruth?" he repeated. "Was that her name? Oh yes, I remember. She was the one that jumped out of the window. Yes. I was very angry about that. I was very angry with her for doing it. I thought she'd escaped punishment. Then it was revealed to me that she had in fact proved her penitence, had truly cleansed herself. I realized then that confession and punishment are preliminary, that death is the one true atonement. There is no other."

Again Norah could only make a gargle of what she wanted to say. Again he understood.

"Victoria? Ah . . . she went easily. She was no trouble. Her sin was great—trying to pass off a bastard as the true son of wedlock. But she acknowledged her guilt and paid her debt. She accepted the ultimate expiation. The other two were headstrong, stubborn, wouldn't admit their transgression. They weren't deceiving me, only themselves, blocking their own road to salvation. But I was sorry for them. My pity was equal to their intransigence. I helped them."

"You killed them!" How she managed to make the words ring out Norah had no idea. She had had to do it for the record, for the tape, and she had done it.

"I helped them," he insisted.

He'd never call it murder, never, never, she realized. It was hopeless. She couldn't make him say it. "They were innocent."

"Guilty! Guilty!" he shouted into the fog. "Sly and guilty as Delilah. The last one, she tried to seduce me. Did you know that? I knocked on her door, and she let me in without question. Oh, she pretended she was expecting someone else, but she was willing anyway. You call that innocence? I call it foul."

That would be Carmen Piñero, Norah thought, the woman who had been killed in her place; poor Carmen Piñero must have tried to distract her killer in the only way she knew. It was best not to let herself dwell on what must have gone on between them—on the pretty widow's pathetic efforts. . . . Oh God, don't let me think about it! As an admission it might be adequate. It would have to be. Norah was too weak, her throat hurt too much to go on. She slumped against him. She was finished.

But he didn't want her that way—he wanted her conscious and cowering. He jerked her back on her feet. "Are you going to be one of the stubborn ones? Well?"

If she could stay conscious till he put her in the water, she might, just might, be able to drift down shore. He wouldn't be able to see beyond the first couple of feet, so he wouldn't know whether or not she was sinking. Anyhow, once out of his reach, what could he do about it? She was a pretty good swimmer, and if the current was not too strong. . . .

"Well?" He shook her and, sensing that she wanted to say something, loosened his hold.

Oh, yes, he wanted to hear her grovel all right. So then she would. "No, I'm not stubborn. I want to be forgiven. I want to repent. I do repent. Please, please, I accept . . . my punishment."

"Ah . . . good . . ."

The ground sloped downward; the slap of water against the shore was unmistakable and close. She tried to remember whether there was bulkheading here or not. Did it matter? In the very next second she found out that it did matter. She was dragged down on the wet grass in such a way that the wooden rim of the shoring cut into her ribs and her head hung out over the lip, facedown. He was going to hold her head under. He had no intention of putting her into the river and letting her go. She would have no chance to swim. She would be drowned almost without getting wet.

Her scream came out a thin, mewling whimper.

"No, no, I can't let you go. You might drift away."

She was crying as this one last hope was torn from her. She tried to remonstrate, to reassure him, and all she could produce were choked, helpless, enraged, sobs of despair.

He would not relent. "No, I'm really sorry, Norah, but once in the water the shock of it might just tempt you to swim. We can't take that risk, can we? Oh, you'll make your own expiation just as I promised. I'll only stand by to protect you from your human frailties, that's all. To give you peace, Norah, that's all I want."

He was cloyingly sincere and eager. The eagerness flowed out of his fingertips in renewed pressure on her abused throat. His voice rose and quavered with his eagerness into an odd high squeak that reminded her . . . not of the voice on the phone, of something else, but of . . . what? No time for analyzing, no time for forcing her memory; whatever strength she had left she must now use in one all-or-nothing attempt to get loose. Lying still so that her effort would be concentrated, Norah raised her arms up and back, reaching for his face. Finding it, she dug her nails into his cheeks as hard as she could.

He seemed scarcely to feel it. He shook her off with a twist of his head and no more than petty annoyance.

"Now, now, Norah . . ." He was actually placating her dying frenzy!

But the scratches would show, oh, yes, they would show. There would be that at least. If she could roll over off her back, then she could raise a knee and put a foot into his stomach as she'd been taught . . . but it was too late; he was pushing her head down, down. Instinctively, Norah held her breath, just in time, for her face felt cold wetness and then her whole head went under. How long would she be able to hold her breath? Already her lungs aching from the restricted breathing of the past minutes were close to bursting. *Dear Lord!* Norah prayed. *Dear Lord, forgive me for all the wrongs of my life; take me to your bosom.*

Unexpectedly and without apparent reason, she was released. She turned her head sideways, gulping for air. Then she was raised and pulled back and placed faceup on the grass. Though she didn't open her eyes, she couldn't bring herself to it yet, she could sense light through the lids. Curiosity was what finally made her look, but she was as blinded in the brilliance as she had been in the dark and the fog. After a while she became aware of sound—voices, distant voices—yet there were dark blurred figures very close by. In fact, her head was now cushioned on somebody's knees. The face that leaned over hers was old, and the sunken cheeks were streaked with rain—or tears.

"Oh, my girl . . . my sweet girl. . . ."

Dad!

"The ambulance is on its way, Mr. Mulcahaney."

It was Dad holding her! She opened her mouth to ask how he had got there, but the mere effort was intolerable.

"Don't try to talk, sweetheart."

Her eyes were growing accustomed to the glare of the spotlights. The double images converged into recognizable faces and forms. That was Lieutenant Felix who had just spoken, and beyond him and her father were Joe, Detective Brennan, and between them in handcuffs a tall man with a kind of white gauze thing across the bottom of his face—a surgical mask, of course, a simple surgical mask! Above it the eyes that stared at her were hostile . . .

"Henry," she whispered.

Now she knew why the voice had sounded muffled, strange, yet familiar. She understood too why he had used the mask, wanting to remain anonymous right to the end, wanting to remain the Avenger.

"Henry!" She cried out in full shock and realization. It was torn from her without conscious will, out of surprise and appalled recognition. The pain it caused her mangled throat was beyond what she could bear.

"What . . . took . . . you . . . so . . . long?"

Propped up against the pillows, her throat still swaddled in wet dressings, Norah slowly rasped out the words one by one.

"Norah!" Her father sitting beside the hospital bed caught her up right away. "Where's your gratitude . . . and your respect?" But the reprimand was automatic, almost absentminded. Now that the lieutenant had arrived, Patrick Mulcahaney was nervous.

"That's all right; it proves she's getting back to normal." Behind Felix's jocularity, he too was uneasy. He covered it with exaggerated sternness. "I thought you were told not to move from the area of the stairs?"

"I didn't intend to . . . I. . . ."

"Sh. . . . Don't talk, listen." Felix exchanged a quick look with Mulcahaney and got an almost imperceptible nod in return. So that meant the old man wanted him to do the explaining. Of course, it was his duty. He had done what had to be done, but Jim Felix in all his years of command couldn't remember feeling as responsible to anyone as he did to this girl. "Why do you think Sorlein decided to visit you last night? Who do you think suggested he drop by?"

There was only one person.... "Dad? Was it you?"

"I asked your father to do it," Felix answered for him. "While you were out during the afternoon marketing, Cap planted bugs in your living room and set up listening equipment down the hall at Mrs. Kelley's. I was there and your father joined us; he never left the building, that is, not till later."

"Dad! All that about baby-sitting me..."

Mulcahaney flushed.

Felix continued. "When I went to your father yesterday he was naturally reluctant to expose you. On the other hand, to let you go ahead and marry a man who might, no matter how slight the possibility, be a psychotic killer would be to put you in jeopardy every minute for the rest of your life."

Patrick Mulcahaney couldn't speak, but he looked at his daughter, pleading for her understanding.

"So your father agreed. He called Sorlein. He put it to Sorlein that he was worried that you'd become interested in another man, someone you'd met recently, probably while you were living alone as Norah Fogarty."

"The way Henry jumped at it ready to believe the worst!" Mulcahaney growled. "To tell the truth that was when I began to have my doubts. For all his fine talk, Henry didn't trust you."

Norah smiled and reached for her father's hand. Mulcahaney squeezed back. He felt easy again. She was his girl now as always—she would understand the rest of what he'd had to do.

Norah meanwhile was trying to sort it out. "When Ellis came up to see me at noon yesterday in the apartment, he left a cigarette in the ashtray. I wasn't sure whether Henry had noticed it."

Felix shrugged. "It's possible he did. It would have prepared him for what your father had to say."

"But why didn't you tell me? Prepare *me?*" She looked from one to the other.

Mulcahaney grimaced. This was the part he'd dreaded, and

this was the part he couldn't leave to the lieutenant to explain. "Lieutenant Felix wanted to do just that, Norah, but I said no." Though she made no move to take her hand away, he instinctively lunged forward as though she had. "I still couldn't believe it about Henry, you see. What I mainly worried about was what would happen if we put the doubt in your mind and then he turned out all right. Would you ever get over it? Would you ever feel right with him again?"

"I guess not."

There was no need for either of them to say more. Patrick Mulcahaney's eyes filled; the tears spilled out, but he wasn't ashamed.

For her father the matter might be closed, but not for Norah. "Suppose I hadn't got rid of Henry? Suppose we'd just sat in the apartment? You could have listened all night and not heard anything useful."

"We didn't expect to hear anything useful—the bugging was a precaution. We had confidence that you'd get rid of Henry so that you could keep the date with Ellis." There was a slight gleam in Felix's eye. "We knew you'd manage it somehow, and that it would increase Sorlein's suspicions. He'd follow you, and I'd follow him. We hoped, of course, that he'd go into the bar after you."

"Oh. But . . . what about Robert? What about Robert Ellis? Why did he call me and then not show?"

"Because that was the way it was planned."

Norah just gaped.

"Since your father didn't want your suspicions of Sorlein aroused, we decided to let you go on thinking Ellis was the guilty one as long as possible. By the way—with Mr. Ellis' apologies." The lieutenant placed a small, neatly wrapped brown paper parcel on her lap.

Norah had no doubt what it was, and she would have given a great deal not to have to open it with both the lieutenant and her father watching. Evidently, the lieutenant sensed her embarrassment over the gun and continued his explanation.

"Robert Ellis turned himself in and is cooperating fully. He's already given us that phone number we wanted; he doesn't know the name that goes with it; but he knows the man, and he's prepared to make identification. We've turned that part of it over to the Narco squad. They're not going to make the collar right away—they want to play out the string, hoping it will lead to a whole network that caters to the executive market."

"He's an addict?" Norah whispered.

"That's it. He became addicted while hospitalized in Saigon after major surgery. Not a new story, this one has a more than usually tragic twist. Seems when he got back to the States, Ellis voluntarily committed himself for treatment and was pronounced cured. So he went home to Michigan City, Indiana, to marry his childhood sweetheart. Two days before the wedding the girl had a routine physical and found out she had cancer . . . terminal in three months. She killed herself. It drove Ellis back to drugs.

"Well, when he found out you were a policewoman, he jumped to the conclusion that you were after him for possession and use. Your having just asked him for that number, which was the one of his supplier, had alerted him. He was nervous and edgy and he panicked. When he got away and had a chance to think it out, he realized not only that the contact with you had been accidental but that the whole setup was much too elaborate to catch a user like himself. Whoever you were after had done something far worse than shooting up horse. Having got that far, Ellis realized that his best bet was to turn himself in." Felix paused. "I think he was glad to have a direct reason to do it. He's going for the cure again, and this time I think he'll stay clean."

Norah sighed.

"What Ellis didn't realize was that his very panic when he

discovered your true identity was a strong indication of his innocence. After all, the man who killed Carmen Piñero already knew you were a policewoman."

That was it! That was the elusive bit of reasoning she'd searched for.

Gently, Felix led her through the steps of it. "We agreed, didn't we, all of us in the squad room yesterday morning, that he must have known from the beginning that you were a decoy, that he went through the motions of harassing you only to fool us. So unless you think that Ellis was putting on an act when he saw your gun and shield . . ."

"No. It was no act."

"Also, of course, by then we were pretty sure it had to be Sorlein."

"When did you guess?"

"Guess, Mulcahaney?" Felix pretended to be appalled. "There's no guessing in policework. We were alerted to the very strong likelihood after the caller made his initial contact with you. You remember the first call came within minutes after Sorlein left the apartment? Now we knew that Ellis wasn't around to see Sorlein go up or come down. Schmidt was tailing Ellis, and Schmidt reports that he waited just long enough to see your lights go on and then went straight home. But the clincher was what the caller said: He accused you of entertaining two men on the same night."

The lieutenant gave her a moment to digest it. "Even if Ellis had spotted Sorlein lurking when he brought you home, even if he had seen Sorlein enter the building, how could he have known that Sorlein was going up to your apartment? If you're going to suggest someone watching from across the street with a spyglass, you can forget it—we checked it out. Only someone who knew you well enough to recognize Sorlein as your boyfriend could have known that you entertained a second man that night. . . or the second man himself." Felix paused and sighed. "We contacted your father right away and found out that you'd only recently started going with Sorlein and that you'd met under . . . uh . . . informal circumstances."

Mulcahaney looked stricken. "I thought I'd picked him up, but it seems it was the other way."

Felix nodded. "He must have spotted Norah . . . let's see, it was after the Neumann case that he turned up, wasn't it? Probably he was watching outside the Neumann house. He liked Norah's looks and decided it would be a good way to keep up with what the police were doing."

"I went to a lot of trouble to make sure he was all right," Mulcahaney told the lieutenant.

"I'm sure you did, Mr. Mulcahaney, and as far as his two years in New York were concerned, there wasn't anything we could find against him either. But we went farther back. He claimed to have come from Hartford, but that turned out to be only a way station. Now why had he offered his future father-in-law a half lie? Of course, it was easy to find out where he really did come from—Taunton, Massachusetts. Cap went up there. It didn't take long to get the story."

That explained Joe's absences right in the middle of the case, Norah thought.

"Sorlein's neighbors in Taunton weren't surprised that a detective should be making inquiries about him. Seems Sorlein had also been engaged to a local girl and then drafted, just like Ellis. When he came back, he discovered not that she'd married someone else, maybe he could have borne that, but that she'd turned into a party girl. Seems everybody in town, and plenty from out of town too, had had her. It made an extra impact on him because of his childhood. Henry's mother had walked out on his father. She was flighty but evidently cared enough about the boy to take him with her. He was only nine, but he had an idea of what was going on. She didn't stay with the new man very long or with any of the others either. When she got older and couldn't be quite so choosy, she settled down again—with a house painter in Taunton. But it wasn't in her to stay put, and this time she left the boy behind. The house painter, who incidentally was very fond of Henry and left him everything, grieved himself into the grave. So. The shock of the girl he loved turning out like his mother was too much. Sorlein called her and, I suppose, poured out his childhood's hate on her. Right after that there was a rash of obscene calls in the town. Nothing could be proved, but the suspicion against Sorlein was very strong. It was made uncomfortable enough for him so that he finally liquidated his stepfather's assets and left.

"He got a good job in Hartford with one of the big insurance companies, stayed away from women—to the extent that his co-workers thought there was something wrong with him, which there was but not what they thought. The rumor got to him, and he was so enraged that he quit and came back to New York.

"Deserved or not, you can't blame a man for being secretive about a reputation like that. However, the pattern did fit the psychological requirements of the man we wanted. Take Ruth Emerson's death. She'd been having an affair with Julio Valdes while her husband was on the road. She was afraid that he'd found out and that his accident was really suicide. Whether it was or not, the caller encouraged her to believe she was responsible and drove her to jump out of her window.

"Victoria Neumann's husband died in combat, but she carried another man's child. Who can say that the caller's taunts drove her to take her own life and the unborn baby's? Who can say that either of those women would or would not have committed suicide if left alone? We do know that Arabella Broome would not have.

"From the beginning Arabella Broome's innate innocence checkmated him. She would not knuckle under. Worse, she actually fought back. That frustration forced him to perform his first overt act. Now he'd found a much more satisfying way of resolving his resentments and hate. He rationalized that he was assisting these Mary Magdalenes to expiate, but he was also developing a taste for the sacrifice.

"So far we were basing our suspicion of Sorlein on his background and the caller's accusation that you had entertained two men on the same night. We'd already established that the caller had no previous knowledge or acquaintance with his other victims, that his taunts were evolved from a careful noting of the husband's obituary plus a diabolical sensitiveness in probing the women's reactions to his hints and suggestions and leading them from one agonized admission to the next till he knew their innermost secrets. Could that accusation against you have been one of those lucky, instinctive probes? But there was no probing in your case; the accusation was instant. I had to stand by my original reasoning that it was either Sorlein or someone so close to you that he recognized Sorlein and also knew that you were a decoy in that apartment."

It was why she'd been sent home. But Norah still didn't understand why the lieutenant had dismissed her so abruptly, in front of the whole squad. She flushed again, remembering the humiliation.

"Who knew you were a decoy?" Felix asked gently.

"Well, Dad, naturally, and Henry. . . ."

"Who else?"

"Nobody." She shrugged. "Except you, of course, Lieutenant, and Sergeant Capretto, and . . . and. . . ." She was too shocked to go on.

"That's right, Mulcahaney . . . and every man in the department." Felix finished for her.

Oh, no! Norah thought. Oh, how awful!

"I've never in my life set a trap and been so anxious to see it sprung." Lieutenant James Felix sighed heavily. "About taking so long to get to you . . . I'm sorry, but between Cap and Brennan and me . . . we were spread pretty thin."

Brennan had been up North for the past ten days cooperating with the Canadian authorities on a case and had returned only the morning after the Piñero homicide. Joe had been sitting with her at the time Carmen Piñero was strangled. They were the only two the lieutenant had dared to trust!

The lieutenant himself had been Henry's tail while Joe and Roy covered her in the bar. Instead of the dozen men she'd thought were spread out along the river there had been only those three. She really was glad she hadn't known!

"So." It was Felix's final punctuation. He got up. "You helped catch a killer that could have terrorized the whole city and you were instrumental in uncovering a new narco network. I'm putting your name in for promotion to detective."

She'd given up even thinking about it, much less hoping, and now here it was—the promotion she'd dreamed about. She flushed with pleasure. Turning to share it with her father, she saw the hard truth in his eyes. "I don't deserve it. I just stumbled my way through."

"You don't need to be that tough on yourself. You showed a lot of courage down there by the river. You got Sorlein to talk, and you got it down on tape."

"Thank you."

"As long as you realize you have a lot to learn."

"Oh, I do, Lieutenant."

"On the other hand, you'll have plenty of teachers; we've never had a woman on the squad before." Then Felix grinned broadly. "I don't suppose I have to worry about your being squelched, though."

There was a knock at the door. A young, crisp student nurse looked in. "You have another visitor," she told Norah and, without waiting for permission, stood aside and beckoned.

Joseph Antony Capretto sauntered in. At the sight of the lieutenant he stopped short, looking sheepish. In his arms was a large bouquet of red roses.